Bernard Ashley

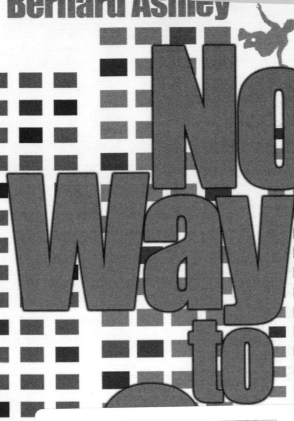

No Way to

ORCHARD BOOKS

ORCHARD BOOKS
338 Euston Road, London NW1 3BH
Orchard Books Australia
Level 17/207 Kent Street, Sydney, NSW 2000

ISBN 978 1 40830239 2

Text © Bernard Ashley 2009

10 9 8 7 6 5 4 3 2 1

Printed in Great Britain

Orchard Books is a division of Hachette Children's Books,
an Hachette UK company.

www.hachette.co.uk

I should like to thank David Ashley, Jonathan Ashley, Luke Ashley, Rose Ashley, Adèle Hagan, Bob Pinkerton, Maria Waters and Paul Williams for their help with my research for this book; and Kirsty Skidmore and Catherine Coe for their brilliant editing.

Chapter One

Amber Long stared into the policeman's face. Her eye shadow and lip gloss made it very clear that she was giving Thames Reach Academy a miss that Friday, which wasn't a drama day with Mr Pewtrell. But they weren't sending the law round to the flats for skivers, were they?

'Mrs Long?' the policeman asked.

Amber snorted. 'Do I look like Mrs Long?' So what game was her stupid father playing in prison, getting her mum a knock-up at nine o'clock in the morning?

'Is Mrs Long in?'

'No, she isn't.' Amber stuck out her jaw. Her mother Debra – *Debs* to her boyfriends – hadn't been home for a couple of nights.

'Do you know where she is, love?'

'Do you know where Osama Bin Laden is?'

'And your father?'

'Ask the governor of Marwood prison.'

The policeman – young and pimply – was breathing deeply, and his face was going blotchy. From his looks this wasn't a cat-and-mouse game he was enjoying, the way some of them would draw things out when it was a half-dressed teenage girl they were talking to. 'I need to see your mother.'

'Well you can't. You'll have to come back.'

The PC looked both ways along the walkway. He glanced down at his radio, but taking another deep breath he came out with it. 'Have you got a younger brother? Connor?'

'He *can't* go to school. He got the boot. No one'll have him.'

'Can I come inside, Miss?'

'You going to get your truncheon out?'

But the young policeman was already taking off his helmet and sliding past her into the narrow passage. As soon as they were in the kitchen, he said, 'I'm afraid I've got bad news.'

'What's that?' But Amber knew the answer as soon as she asked. She was bright. It wouldn't be her father, and it wouldn't be her mother – he'd asked where they were. And when he'd mentioned her brother he'd said his name. It had to be Connor.

'Your brother . . . Connor Long . . . he's dead.' The policeman reached out a hand to her shoulder but didn't touch. 'He's fallen off a balcony over at Riverview House. Paramedics said he died on impact. He didn't suffer, love.'

And Amber crumpled, not onto a chair but down onto the floor. 'The silly little toe-rag!' she shouted into the tiles. 'Oh, the silly little fool!' But straight off she was kneeling up again. 'No – he couldn't!' she screamed at the policeman. 'He wouldn't! Not my Connor! He's too good a climber! He'd never fall off anything!'

Up west, a rough-haired youth with a drained face shivered on the pavement, awkwardly holding the sign pointing to 'BEST SEATZ – TOP THEATRE TICKETS FOR TODAY'; while in his warm office above the ticket agency Radu Noica sat at a desk covered with a sheet of glass, beneath which was a map of London's theatres. On top of the glass were listings magazines and a file of auditorium seating plans. On the walls were plans of Wembley Arena, the Hammersmith Apollo, the O_2, and posters from current shows – mainly musicals. It looked like a typical ticket agency operation, which was the point, because although theatre tickets were sold to tourists downstairs, Radu Noica was really about something else altogether. The phone he mostly used wasn't either of the two landlines on his desk but one of the mobiles in his pockets – while beneath the glass the map that really counted was the second sheet, spread beneath the theatre chart, visible with a quick lift. This was the map of Greater London where certain territories were marked in colour: blue for himself, the Romanian Noica operating on the north side of the Thames, and yellow for the South London suppliers – both territories drawn over with the changing jigsaw of the others, the Somalis, the Yardies, the Triads, and the British Boys. What he knew about the people who bought the drugs he imported was coded, and locked away in his safe.

Noica was listening to a message on one of his mobiles. He was a lean man, with a shaven head, heavy brows, watery eyes, bloodless lips, and a voice of the cold sea. 'Understand.' With no expression on his face, he snapped his mobile shut and leaned over to a 1950s Mayfair phone on which he dialled an outside number. 'Get him this message. Nothing. He says nothing, understand? He must not forget he has family.' He thumped the phone cradle to end the call, before buzzing an extension downstairs. 'Get me one ticket for the James Bond film,' he said. 'Opening. Tonight. As well you have my photograph taken, Noica all top of the world, going into Empire Theatre . . .' Although from the tone of his voice he could still have been making threats.

Dimitris Papendreou's Hertfordshire home sat sprawled along the Cockfosters Road. Two gates opened onto a curved gravel path leading to the front entrance of *Acropolis*. Pillars, porticos, a double garage, huge windows and stone lions spelt out wealth – and power, with the automatic gates, the guard dog, the swivelling security cameras and the tinted windows daring anyone to enter the property without good reason. But

the Greek who owned it was not an imposing figure –
no tall, tanned Theseus who might lift one of his own
stone lions. 'Mr P' was slight, bald, and around sixty;
his black-framed glasses seemed the most striking
thing about him. Behind them, though, there was
a stillness, a stare, a suit that dare not crease, the
expensive skin of a powerful man; and there were never
any raised voices or uninvited comment when he was
in the room.

Right now he was in his study, which was at the side
of the house where the sun spread itself across
a splendid mosaic marble floor. He was alone at his
long desk, with just a telephone and a demitasse of
Greek coffee. He was listening to someone making
a report, taking notes in a small leather book.

'So,' Dimitris Papendreou said, 'Croydon is up thirty,
Brighton is up twenty-three, but a big loss in Piccadilly
. . .' His informant told him about a punter's lucky run
on one of the roulette tables. 'So you axe the croupier.
There's no such thing as a long run of luck in Aristotle
Casinos . . . So now what's with the bookie shops and
the smaller stuff, on the streets?' This time he was told
things that made him nod with some satisfaction. 'And
the football player in Marwood Prison? He can no
longer exercise every day?' When he heard his man's
response he retained his stillness, simply pursing his
lips. 'Why are some messages so hard to get across?
I want a result. Get onto it.' And he replaced the phone

in its holder, just as his daughter Ariadne brought him another coffee.

'This is fresh,' she told him, 'hot and strong.'

He looked up at her. 'It needs to be.' He patted her on the backside, twinkled behind his thick glasses. 'Can you believe – I am being disobeyed by a man who owes me?'

'No, I don't believe it!'

'But not for long.' He drank his coffee in one hot gulp – and watched the shadow on the marble floor as the sun withdrew.

It was the usual scene. The police tape fluttering, the neighbours staring, the blue lights flashing, the photographers and reporters moving about. And within half an hour the first tribute flowers would be laid against the wall. Dermot Mark of BBC London News was there with a trainee assistant and a sound-camera operator, the first shot they agreed on being a pan of the fall down Riverview House. Fourteen floors. Later on, he'd send Sunil Dhillon to go knocking on doors to ask for a recent photograph of the young victim.

The police incident officer had been as helpful to the media as he could. 'A young white boy, around ten years of age, fell to his death from a high balcony at Riverview House at approximately nine am this morning. At this moment in time we don't know the exact floor he fell from, but we presume it would be the tenth, where a boy his age was seen earlier. He died immediately. A further statement will be made from Thames Reach police headquarters at a time to be advised. Thank you, ladies and gentlemen.'

'Should he have been in school?'

'Was he in school uniform?'

'Where's he been taken?'

'Is his mother with him?'

'Inspector, any details of witnesses?'

'Can you name him?'

'Address?'

The uniformed inspector waved a polite but firm hand. 'We have yet to inform his next of kin. 020 8854 1212. Ring us there and we'll give you the conference details, later today.'

Dermot Mark scribbled the number in his book. 'Another kid's death. No knife this time, no gun – but we could make the national news with this.'

Steve switched off the camera. 'I'll get some general shots, and go up to the top balcony for an aerial. Give us a call if you get anyone for an interview; the OB unit's coming. Otherwise, ring in and see if they want us to cover the police station shout . . .' He was director as well as sound-camera operator.

'OK, I'll stick around here . . .'

Steve went off, and Sunil was about to follow the inspector to the incident van when a loud wailing suddenly silenced the Barrier Estate.

'Connor! *Connor!* Who's done this? What've you been up to?' Along the pavement Amber Long pushed a PC aside, ducked under the tape, and ran to where an officer was photographing a chalked outline on the concrete. It looked like a cartoon of a kid asleep. '*Connor!*' she screamed, kneeling and pummelling the ground with her fists – raising her head to shriek '*No!*' at the tower block.

Sunil Dhillon, the trainee reporter, wrote *Connor* in his notebook.

The evidence officer cased his camera. 'Excuse me, miss . . .' He put a hand towards her.

'I'm his sister!'

'I'm very sorry.'

The PC who had been pushed aside was with them now, helping his colleague lift Amber gently to her feet, passing her over to a female officer. 'OK, OK, love, Susan'll take care of you.'

'Yeah – come on, sweetheart.' The officer led Amber to where a colleague poured a mug of coffee from a flask. 'Were you the only one at home?'

Sunil Dhillon leaned as close to the tape as he was allowed.

'Yeah.'

'And what's your name?'

'Amber. Amber Long.'

Sunil wrote *Long* in his notebook.

'Is your mother coming?'

'She's not there.'

'Where is she, Amber?'

'Out. Dunno.'

The inspector had come over and was nodding, followed by Dermot Mark who no longer had a camera available. 'I'm very sorry,' the inspector was saying. 'Tragic. Would you be prepared to come down to the station and give us some more details? Get away from here . . .'

Amber stared at him. Couldn't the man understand? 'I don't *want* to get away from here! Not yet. Then I want to see him.' Determined, no buts. She handed back her mug, pulled out her mobile phone, and tapped in eleven fast digits. Her mother changed phones the way she changed her knickers – but this just might get to her . . .

'Is that your mother you're calling?'

Amber snapped the phone shut. *Number not recognised.* She sat on the low wall, along from the reporters.

'Let me know when you're ready and you can go in a car with the detective constable there.' The inspector nodded towards a young man in a cheap suit.

Amber stared at him, through him. Who could she trust? What did she dare say to anyone? Because she knew something they didn't. She knew something that opened up a whole different can of worms. *She knew without doubt that Connor had not slipped.* Her

15

kid brother had been deliberately pushed, murdered. Some villain had killed him. When he was little, Connor had climbed before he walked – over the side of his cot, up into his high chair; and then as an infant up onto the garages at the back of the flats. From the off, being somewhere high was like a drug to Connor: the flat roof of the nursery, then the school, the community centre, the steep church; and there was nothing that gave him more of a laugh than some do-gooder turning out the fire brigade to save him; by which time he'd come down another way. He was king at it. Take him to Everest and he'd be up it like a shot – in flip-flops and a blindfold, if asked. So Riverview House with its window ledges and balconies and satellite dishes was a breeze to a climber like Connor. If he'd bothered with Riverview House that morning – and why in hell would he, with all the other new stuff being built around here? – he'd no more come off it than someone lying in bed would suddenly fall out for no reason. No. He'd been pushed, or thrown. There was murderous stuff going on! Amber's eyes were dry now, and clear.

'Sunil Dhillon, BBC TV,' Sunil started, from along the wall. 'I'm very sorr—'

'No – *I'm* sorry, sir!' the inspector interrupted, putting himself between Amber and the trainee. 'You know the form.' And he organised the reeling out of more incident tape, and the shunting back of the media.

The young detective in the suit had walked over.

'I can understand you wanting to stay for a bit', he said to Amber. 'Don't come before you're ready.'

Amber was caught on a sudden intake of breath. *Wanting to stay for a bit?* She shouldn't be here in the first place! She should be at the O_2 getting tickets for Half Past Yesterday! That was the real world. This was untrue! Crazy stuff! *Connor – DEAD?* What rubbish was that? What she wanted to be doing was cuddling him, and tickling him, and bouncing his bony body on the bed till the springs went, working him up to those shrieks and screams that always got their mum shouting. Connor Long was Amber's baby brother – he'd always been: he was special – not some chalk outline on the ground . . .

So, yes, she wanted to stay for a bit – where he'd died.

They found Debra Long: with a male friend, Winston, standing smoking outside A Cuppa Coffee in Lewisham High Street. At the police station Amber had come up with some names her mother sometimes mentioned – one of which rang a bell with the detective constable, who'd arrested the guy three months before. This led him to Winston's flat, where Winston's pregnant girlfriend pointed them in the direction of Lewisham.

At the first sight of the law coming towards them Debra and Winston shifted to go; but it could only be back into the coffee shop, so they faced it out.

'Debra Long?' the female officer asked.

'What?'

'Well, I'm very sorry, Debra – but I need a word. Do you want to come over to the car . . .?'

Winston looked at his watch. 'Gotta go, Debs. I'm serious late, babe.' And he went.

Debra trod on her cigarette and went with the officer and the young plain-clothes man, over to the police car at the kerb. The woman in uniform got into the back with her.

'It's Connor, isn't it? You've pulled him for putting in a car window or something.'

'I'm sorry to tell you –' a hand on her shoulder 'he's dead, Debra. He's had a fatal fall . . .'

'Oh.'

No shriek. No tears. No head slumped onto her chest or raised to heaven. Debra simply stared ahead. At which the DC in the front of the car switched on the ignition and drove them towards Thames Reach and the King George VI Hospital: where Amber and another female officer were waiting for them, round at the back in the mortuary area.

Amber saw her mother get out of the car, still wearing the straight black coat she'd put on to go out three days before. 'They told you? You know about Connor?'

'Yes.' Short, terse, dry-eyed as Debra hugged her daughter – but not for comfort, more like a handshake. 'You seen him?'

'Wouldn't let me, till you got here. Once they'd found you.'

'Yeah, well . . .' Debra turned to the young man in the suit. 'I'm here, aren't I?' She held her head erect, the modern haircut only slightly blown, leaving a strand across her left eye. She still looked young, considering the drink and stuff she did. Smelt a bit smoky, that was all.

'This way.' The DC's voice was low and soft, had been for everything he'd said to Amber. They went inside the mortuary where in the centre a small body on a trolley lay covered with a purple shroud. The mortuary attendant in his dark suit went to its head.

Amber found it hard to breathe. The air in there smelt of a mix of disinfectant and incense; but it wasn't that: it was the sickening fact that little Connor was dead. He would never again go out on one of his climbs, or sneak indoors with a pirate DVD, or bring her a vodka-kick, or bust his bed in a play fight. Amber couldn't even swallow – and she thought she might throw up. But somehow she held on – for Connor.

'Don't worry, love, he looks OK,' the attendant said quietly, reaching for the shroud and slowly drawing it back.

Oh God, wouldn't it be great if it was some other kid? What if they'd made a mistake? If it could only be some other kid – just not her Connor!

But there lay Connor Long, ten years, three months,

and two days old, cropped dark hair, eyes closed, looking the way Amber would see him some mornings when she rousted him out of his bed. Except this morning he'd woken early – and gone to sleep seventy years too bloody soon . . .

It was the holding of breath that could be heard. Until Debra spoke. 'Yes, that's him,' as if she were in some other reality. 'That *was* him.' And she turned away and walked out of the mortuary like a figure in a jerky film.

Amber stood staring at her brother as the shroud was replaced – and didn't feel the DC's comforting hand on her arm. Now she swallowed; and vowed to herself that Connor Long wasn't going to be in the past to her – the fact that he'd ever lived and been her brother was going to be the future. Because she knew right now, standing here, that she was never going to sleep peacefully again until she knew who had pushed this climbing boy who would never have slipped.

Chapter Two

Marwood's town centre traffic system could be clearly heard from the governor's office in the eighteenth-century prison – every engine rev and impatient beep was a reminder of the world outside. 2703145 Prisoner Long was standing blowing out his cheeks in front of the sharp woman in a Jacquel suit, his head on one side, asking the question – *what's this for?* Long knew that him being a category B prisoner, this sudden parade could mean a job in a different workshop, a wing change, or a transfer to some other prison, just to shake things up. Or it could be the governor wanted to know something about another con, not that she'd be lucky there. Or it could be bad news. All ways up, it wasn't a parade he wanted – unless it meant a transfer out of here one day soon.

He stood to what passed for attention – heels loosely together, hands hanging at his sides and eyes reluctantly making contact across the desk. He was thirty-four, had fathered Amber at seventeen when Debra was still at school, and still looked more like a shifty kid than a dad. On those eyes alone he would never be a 'trusty' who was allowed to make the governor's tea. He jerked his head at her; sort of, *what?*

It was bad news. The governor looked to the email and read out the statement she'd received from the incident officer at Thames Reach – bare facts about the fall and the death which, now that all of Connor's immediate family knew, meant that the boy's name could be used in news reports.

Jonny Long swore, looked about to spit on the floor, but twisted round at the prison officer behind him as if it was this man's fault that he was banged up in the nick instead of keeping his boy safe. He flapped his arms helplessly against his sides while the governor signed, dated and timed the statement.

'Keep yourself in line and we'll let you go to the funeral,' she ended, looking up.

Long said nothing. Without permission, he turned and faced the door.

'Right, march off!' the prison officer said. And the governor's painful duty was over, always helped by not being too sympathetic. No prisoner liked walking along the landings with eyes red from crying.

In Thames Reach, DC Webber – 'The name's Ian' – was escorting Amber to the hospital car park, and was going to give her a lift back to Bartram House in his unmarked car. He would have taken her mother, too, but she couldn't be found; she wasn't dodging among the vehicles and she wasn't standing at the bus stop, either. Walking, it would take her a good half hour to get home.

Amber Rose Long was seventeen – sleek dark hair, green eyes, and the bone structure of a Rodin sculpture. Unlike her mother she held herself well, didn't smoke, and to get her laughing and jumping on a night out all she needed were two Vodka Breezers, not six. She was fun enough. In spite of having a delinquent mother and a father in prison – whom she missed like malaria – she was bright, and made the most of life. She'd got enough 'A' to 'C' passes at GCSE to keep the school happy – with 'A's in Drama and English – but the same as a lot of her mates, school never stopped her enjoying a good night out at Camden Koko or Brixton Academy.

But all that was in another life. She sat in the front of Ian Webber's Vauxhall, not interested in the bits and pieces of radio stuff that said this was used as a police car. All she could see was Connor's face back there in the mortuary, with that bruise on his cheek they thought she hadn't spotted, covered with a bit of clever make-up. She didn't want to think what the back of his head was like, or his arms and legs. Under that cover he had to be broken like a dropped phone – shattered.

The car pulled onto the Barrier Estate and stopped outside Bartram House.

'What floor?' Ian Webber asked.

'I'll go up on my own.'

'As you like. Will you be all right? Is your mother coming back soon?'

'Doubt it.' In fact, Amber was pretty sure she wasn't. Debs' reaction to bad stuff was to take something for it – and Amber wasn't thinking Anadin Extra. She'd go into Thames Reach and find a pub where she hadn't been barred . . .

'Want me to send a WPC around? Or is there an aunt, or a gran, or a neighbour you want me to call?'

Amber shook her head. 'I'll manage.' She desperately wanted to be on her own. She wanted to go into Connor's room and make his bed – because the lazy little bugger wouldn't have made it himself – then she wanted to throw herself down on top of it and cry her eyes out. She wanted to find a picture of him – and she knew the one, the day out at Margate, him standing on her shoulders in the sea like a circus kid, just before he dived off backwards. Wherever she went from now on she wanted that picture in her pocket.

'I'm sorry, Amber. A tragic accident,' the DC said.

And in spite of herself, in spite of her gut caution at ever letting anything out to the law, Amber snorted.

Ian Webber turned his head to stare at her. 'You don't think so? You think . . . he might have . . . *jumped*?'

Amber froze. This guy was sharp. She mustn't even *think* anything in this car. She was shocked – but not at what he'd said. It was at herself, for not having thought it. Connor *jump*? It hadn't been anywhere in her head. She found the car door handle, and her stomach suddenly turned over in a terrible twist of truth. A million years was how long he would be dead, which was only the start of it. And in all the years of eternity, the 'for ever' of the world, her little brother had been entitled to just ten. Which was the fiercest fact of all.

But, *jumped*?

She got out of the car. Already word was around, people were about on the landings, leaning over the walkways. Faces. Eyes. And she could imagine some of the quiet words slipping from the sides of those mouths.

Serve him right.

It had to happen one day.

Poor little devil! – but a bloody nuisance all the same.

Father in prison. And where was his mother?

That's no way to go.

Or, perhaps, *Gone to a better world.*

Amber deliberately took the stairs, to show herself on every landing up to the seventh, let people see her with her head held straight, even though she couldn't hold it high. Because whatever they were like, her mum and dad, they were Longs, and she was a Long, and Connor had been a Long.

And this Long was going to find out what really happened. And if it was something needing sorting, then Amber Long was going to be the one to sort it.

*

The BBC was on her doorstep as she reached to door. 'Sunil Dhillon,' the trainee reporter said.

'You said before.'

'I'm sorry to have to come and ask—'

'Ask what?' Amber put the key in the lock, but she wouldn't turn it till the guy had backed off. She wasn't having him pushing inside after her, the way reporters did.

'For a photograph. Of Connor. One you like – they'll put one up in the bulletins, and it might as well be one you like.'

She faced him. This was a job to him; like the man in the mortuary, reporters could hold their faces straight. She'd seen those pictures on the news, often school photographs. 'Well, Connor didn't go to school, so he never had one taken.' And no way would this man see the one of Connor on her shoulders, and her in her bikini. 'Haven't got one.'

'Ah.' He half turned, came back. 'Don't think I like asking, because I don't. I'll tell them you were out . . .'

Now Amber frowned at him. He was a nice-looking boy, young, tallish, Asian with shiny black hair – he would never have pushed after her through the door, she decided. And not a bit like some of the hard old cases who'd pestered her mum when her dad was arrested.

'It's my first assignment on the road – with Dermot Mark.'

She knew the name, and the face: a tall blond guy.

'He's calling up the OB unit.'

'"OB"?' Did she care? But she'd asked.

'Outside Broadcast. BBC London News. You know, the big satellite dish on the van, all that.'

Poor little Connor. Had got them sending a big satellite dish dish – when he was dead!

'I can't promise Dermot won't come and ask . . .'

Amber hesitated. 'Hold on. I'll see what I can dig out.' Get this reporter off her back, she told herself, then she'd shut and bolt the door. Because she'd thought of a picture that would do. It was either that, or them knocking the door down later, or raking round the school he'd been excluded from, or the juvenile court who had to have a mug-shot on their files, so it was going to be something worth showing. She shut the front door on the BBC man and went into her bedroom, where there was a picture Connor took of himself at Christmas, smiling into the new mobile he was holding at arm's length. Self-portrait. She picked it up from her bedside table and took it to the front door. 'Here you are! And tell them he didn't slip, he was too good for that.'

'You don't think so?'

'I know so. And I want that picture back.'

'I'll give you a receipt.'

'You won't. You'll clear off and leave me in peace. But if that doesn't come back, I'll come and find you!'

'Be nice,' Sunil Dhillon said, smiling. 'That'd be nice.'

'Clear off!'

And he went.

When Billy Dawson went anywhere it was in the back of a year-old Jaguar S-type in British racing green, top of the range. His south London nightclub Midnight Express was greatly sought after—literally. The venue changed every year or so from these premises to that, always in cheap-to-rent buildings awaiting development or demolition. This legitimate business kept both him and the police on their toes – he couldn't be relied on to be anywhere for sure, not even at his Georgian house in the Kent village of Meopham, handy for the A2. He slept all over the southeast – but between his current club and the places he reconnoitred for the next Midnight Express, he always travelled in his Jag, driven by Denzel Benjamin, his minder, a big West Indian who was handy with any tool they carried in the boot.

Today Denny was driving Dawson along the Lower Greenwich Road, happening to pass by the Barrier Estate in Thames Reach. At the sight of police tapes and flashing blue Dawson gave a quick eyes-right through the tinted window as Denny drove on past, his car's needle precisely on the speed limit.

'Something gone off there?' he asked his driver.

Denny shrugged. 'Talked to my bruvver – don' affect us.'

'Good.' And Billy Dawson – skinny-faced and head on

one side, looking like a back-slash – resumed clipping his nails onto the Jaguar carpet. Denny would hoover it up later.

Amber didn't know what to do. With herself, that was. She knew what to do about the nosy neighbours along the landing, and about the phone that rang all the time. She ignored them all. No one in this world could have anything to say to her that she wanted to hear. If there'd been the slightest chance it was the hospital calling to say they'd made a mistake, Connor had been in a coma all the time, he'd miraculously come back to life – God, she'd have been sitting by the phone. But she knew that wasn't going to happen. Connor was gone. No one went that cold in a coma, his face had been like stone. In the flat she'd done what she wanted: made his bed, had her cry, and dug out the photo she wanted to have with her always. She'd drawn the curtains against the outside, and drunk so much coffee she'd run out of it and had to go onto tea. And now she sat, staring through the kitchen window, across to where Riverview House was a block-but-one away, knowing what else she wouldn't do. She wouldn't switch on the television. She didn't want to see any local news with her Connor a 'story' on it. In fact, there wasn't anything in life she ever wanted to see or do again except find his killer.

Her dad had never treated Connor right. OK, he loved

him in his own stupid way – knocked about with him when he wasn't off on one of his 'jobs', never showed him any of the violence he was known for: Jonny Long the hard case who'd nut as soon as look. They'd go to Rotherhithe Market and buy daft things, togs to wear and silly gadgets that broke first time they were used. They'd watch football on Sky and Setanta, betting between themselves on who scored, and who won, and who swapped his shirt with whom at the end. Because their dad lived his life at that level – till he'd gambled once too often, fallen foul of someone harder in trying to dig himself out, and gone down for five. But he'd been too stupid to see that Connor didn't need some 'big brother' dad to hero-worship, he needed someone with a bit of common sense to look up to, not kick in the shin when he didn't get what he wanted. Their dad would just ward him off like a spiteful dog that doesn't bite indoors; or he'd laugh; when being the father was what was needed.

As for their mum . . . Well, she'd fallen for a baby as soon as their dad first looked at her, and that had been her, Amber. And she'd spent the rest of Amber's life still trying to be a girl herself – clubbing, drinking, doing drugs – in the middle of which she fell for Connor one drunken night, and she was stuck with him, because their dad wouldn't even think about an abortion. So she didn't give the boy much time – and Connor became Connor.

But Amber had loved him. She'd loved him properly.

If he ever had something nice to eat, it was Amber who'd cooked it. If he wore the sort of trainers he wanted, it was Amber bullying her dad or her mum to get them for him, or buying them herself out of her holiday job money. And when the second school kicked him out, it was Amber who went round and ran a key along both sides of the headteacher's car, front to back and over the boot. It was Amber who cared. And Amber who right now in her grief wasn't going to give anyone the time of day; no one except her Connor. Because there was thinking to do. Her little brother wasn't going to be shuffled off out of this life with the story that he'd slipped, and served himself right. He had never slipped, no chance. And *jumped*? If he was scared out of his mind and he'd jumped, then it was the same as being pushed, wasn't it? No way would he have committed suicide. Someone had done it. And Amber knew that she was going to find out who that was. Police, reporters, no one except her would bother after a couple of days. When the TV lights get switched off and the police files are stuffed into their drawers, it's people like her who are left to go on living with the tragedy.

And with the anger.

Yes, always the anger.

Chapter Three

Jonny Long's cell was a narrow two-up. The furniture was fairly modern, but not much could be done about the narrow window cut through the rag-stone wall, its meagre light about the only thing the two prisoners shared in there. Everything else was territory – my bunk, my chair, my cupboard, my half of the table: my bit of floor to clean, my day for the sink and taps and wiping down the door. With someone else it might be different, but Frank Lodge on the lower bunk was a small, quiet man who said little and shared next to nothing, not even what was on his mind. He was in for arson at a car dealer's who'd sold him a highly polished heap – and then wouldn't give him his money back when the wheels came off. He was private, bitter, obsessed, serving his time till he could get out and at the fly-boy again. He probably didn't even know the man banged-up with him was called Jonny. He certainly never wanted any amusement like betting on a fly landing on this wall, or that; or a talk about the horses running at York; or a bit of arm wrestling to keep their muscles firm. Anyway, the man's brain was dead to any thought except his revenge in three years' time.

Jonny Long had been put away after a serious assault on a London City Airport baggage handler. Violence was in his genes, but the vice he'd grown into was gambling, and what kept him awake most nights was the price he still had to pay – and the man he had to pay it to: a London Greek whose grip could reach through prison walls, a tyrant who ruled by making examples of those who didn't pay up. *Dimitris 'Punish' Papendreou – 'Mr P'.* And Jonny Long was one of those who still owed him. Not in a big way, compared to the sort of debts run up in a Papendreou casino in the West End or Brighton or Croydon. But it's the smaller stuff the local punter gets to hear about, the unpaid debts on the backroom poker and the race nights; because no one looks more stupid than a man owed money who isn't getting paid. So word goes out; and an arm is broken, a face slashed, or a shot fired; and the word on the street is that it's a punishment: then people don't mess with Dimitris Papendreou. They pay up next time.

Not that Papendreou could ever be linked with crimes against the person on the estate walkways and in the backstreets of south London. He lived nowhere near the terraced houses and the high-rise flats, but among MPs and show-biz names and fat-cats in the northern suburbs. How could such a man have anything to do with the smashed kneecaps of a baggage handler from London City Airport?

Papendreou told someone who told someone who had the job done. So it could be in the street, in a flat, behind a supermarket, in a prison – no one was safe anywhere: not if they owed Papendreou. And sometimes, if a beating-up in a prison shower wasn't enough, then the punishment could be transferred outside, to a loved one. And the trouble was, Jonny Long was a Mr P man gone wrong. Known as being hard, to help pay his gambling debts he'd said he'd do what needed doing around the estates; but when he'd been caught and sentenced for GBH, his debt still hadn't been fully paid up, and he'd been given his target inside: a jack-the-lad footballer on a drink-driving death charge, who owed Papendreou a lot more than a week's Premier League wages. A nasty slip down the clattering stairs of E block; or a dropped weight to make history of his metatarsals – it was left to Jonny Long what to do, but it had to be professional and serious enough to hit the press outside. People had to know that Arsenal's Burt Foord was as vulnerable to punishment as any of the punters who played poker in a Mr P game. But if an avenger didn't deliver, then for the benefit of the whole Papendreou set-up, that man had to be dealt his own justice. And Jonny Long hadn't delivered. He'd been told what he had to do in messages from 'friends' and on two visits by Debra – half-cut and not really knowing what she was passing on – but he hadn't done it. Burt Foord could still pass a cool ball in recreation time – and that was something he wasn't supposed to be able to do any more.

Jonny's excuse was that he just hadn't had the chance to do something serious without being the obvious hit man – while Mr P expected him to do the job and take the rap, serve the extra time: it all added to his power. If only Jonny could talk to a chaplain, or a sympathetic prison officer. But there was no one he could trust – and, if he decided to talk on the record, they definitely didn't give out fresh identities to the likes of him. Mr P had got him where he wanted; and Mr P could punish hard . . .

Debra came home eventually. Amber wasn't in bed – she would never sleep again – and she heard her mother's key scraping all around the lock trying to find the hole. It took three minutes, which is a long time when you're lying on the settee deciding whether or not you're going to go and open the door. But when the language got louder and more extreme, she went.

'Get in here!'

Her mother looked terrible. Her hair was pinned back off her face to keep it out of her drink, her mascara had run, and her face was fluttering. She stank of tobacco, reeking off her like a poisonous fog, and the smile she put on – the pathetic attempt at sisters-in-it-together – was nauseating. She'd lost her coat somewhere, her polyester dress was stained, and beneath it her bra was half-on, half-off.

'Been out doing some grieving?'

'Amb – I can't take it in. Tell me it's not true . . .' Debra was leaning all over Amber, who had to take a step back to set her feet more firmly.

'It's true all right.'

Debra found a wail from deep down, riding on a hiccup. 'My little boy! My poor little soldier! What's he . . . what's he . . . done to deserve that?'

'Nothing. He's not done anything. Strewth! – go and wash your face, rinse your mouth, clean your teeth . . .'

'He's done nothing . . . has he . . . to deserve that?' Debra leant against the passage wall. 'Oh, my poor little . . .' she started to slide down it.

'Connor.' That probably hadn't been what her mother had been searching for, but it fitted the situation – this stupid, drunken woman who'd only ever lived for herself, still acting like some selfish teenager.

'Get to the sink.' Amber pulled her mother to her feet and shuffled her along to the bathroom. She'd be sick in a minute – and Amber knew who'd have to do the cleaning up.

'I never said goodbye to him this morning . . .'

'You weren't here.'

'No? Where was I?'

Amber didn't bother to reply. Her mother deserved nothing but her head held under a shower, her clothes pulled off her and a towel thrown in. Let her come to in her own time, out of Amber's reach, who'd like nothing better right now than to smack the stupid woman round the head.

Except – 'I've lost my little boy . . .' Debra groaned, '. . . an' I never really had him, did I?' – and the look she gave Amber, just for a split second, seemed to say that some sliver of grief was actually piercing her heart.

Sunil Dhillon sat at his computer station in the BBC newsroom, having written the first draft of Dermot Mark's report of Connor Long's death for the local news at six-thirty. Next, Mark had done a heavy edit on Sunil's script, and put in his trademark tragic *why?* at the end. Dermot Mark could go to the funeral of a celebrity ninety-nine year old and still ask *why?* – with that fake-bewildered shake of his head. And while it was Sunil who'd borrowed the photograph of Connor Long – looking so alive with that joke of a self-portrait – it was Dermot Mark who had stood in front of it in the studio, and looked at it over his shoulder like a sad relative at a memorial service.

Sunil clicked on an icon to call up the ten-thirty stories in their likely running order. He was on stand-by until the late transmission; his shift finished at the end of the bulletin; done. But when he saw the Connor Long story on the schedule again, he opened up his internet connection to code-in the police website that was accessible to a reputable broadcaster through the Yard press office. He entered 'Connor Long' and read the bare bones of what the incident officer had said at the scene, and had announced later at the press conference. And there at the bottom of the page was a link in blue: *post mortem report*. He clicked on it, and read it all, the background notes and the examination of the body, following its transfer from the hospital. And with a quick intake of breath and a sharp look around the newsroom, he clicked *print*.

The medical details were what he would have expected. He'd have to look up some of the technical terms in a medical dictionary, but there were no surprises in the gist of what he read. Connor's skull had been fractured, both legs broken, and his ribs had caved in, causing internal bleeding. So much for the internal examination; while the external examination described a 'slightly under-nourished male child of ten years; height four feet, three inches, weight sixty-three pounds'. But it was the paragraph headed *Circumstances* that held his interest. It read: 'From the statement of Inspector 4931 Bennett I understand that the body was found at the foot of Riverview House, a fourteen-storey block of flats on the Barrier Estate in Thames Reach, south London. The disposition of the body was consistent with a fall from a great height. The body was clothed in jeans, sweatshirt, and hooded jacket appropriate to age, with 'jockey' underpants and sleeveless vest. The feet were clad in short white socks and 'Spiv' trainers, the left trainer tied with blue laces, and the right trainer tied with red. The child wore no watch, jewellery or piercings, and there were no tattoo marks on the body, either temporary or permanent, nor any recent scars.'

Sunil read this through again, and frowned – and after a quick search in a directory he was telephoning Amber Long on the listed BT number for 'Long, J.' in Bartram House.

'Yes?'

'Amber, it's Sunil Dhillon.'

'Have you still got my photo?'

'Sure.' It's on the BBC system. I can let you have the original back. I wondered if I could meet you . . .?'

'Put it through my letter box.'

'OK – it's just, there's something I wanted to ask you . . .'

'Oh, yeah?' Deliberately the south London *oh, yeah?* that asks all sorts of questions.

Sunil Dhillon coughed, nothing medical, just a hesitation. 'Background. This isn't an open and shut case, I don't think.'

'"Open and shut case"? You're not police.'

'I'm a trainee investigative reporter . . .'

'You want to make your name, do you? Your own little "bong" on News at Ten?'

'Definitely not. And my name wasn't on tonight's news – I'm just an assistant. But you said Connor wouldn't slip – and yet he fell . . .'

'You still fall, don't you, whether you slip, jump, or get pushed . . .?'

'Which is why I want to meet you.'

Amber thought for a moment. This Sunil had been decent earlier; if he was coming on to her he was playing a very crafty game. 'Where, then?'

'Greenwich Park. It's not too far for you but it's off the estate, and it's on my way in to work . . .'

'Tomorrow, you mean.'

'Uh-huh.'

'Whereabouts?'

'Outside the Observatory – opposite, there's a stall selling spicy sausages.'

Amber knew it. 'When?'

'About eight? Give you time to get to college after.'

'I might be there.' They exchanged mobile numbers, and Amber put down the phone because the entry buzzer had just sounded. But she'd meant what she'd said – she might or she might not turn up.

Shock. 'Hi, Amber. It's Dawn Feldman.' The deputy head at Amber's school – quickly invited up, and like seeing your mother in the form room; although Amber knew her mostly from outside school. Mrs Feldman was a local councillor who organised the school holiday booster courses at Charlton Athletic football ground – and who'd got Amber and her friend Lauren their juice-and-biscuits jobs. Dawn Feldman had kids of her own and a street tongue, was all over the school as if there were ten of her. Trouble in the canteen? Somehow she was in there before it kicked off. At the school gates?

Before or after school, she was on patrol: and parents parking on the zig-zags moved off quicker for her than they did for any traffic warden.

And here she was on Amber's doorstep at half-nine in the evening.

'Amber . . .'

'Oh. Hi. Yeah. You want to come in?'

'Only if it's OK. I've got to be at the bottom of your list of people you want to see right now.' She had a local ring to her voice that went down well at Thames Reach Academy.

'No. Come in.' Debra had gone to bed after being sick, she'd be 'out' till tomorrow afternoon; and there'd been enough Dettol to cover the smell. And thank goodness Amber's dad liked the flat kept up to the mark, and it stayed that way; the grot was in Debra's mind, not her home.

They went into the small front room, which Dawn Feldman filled with a presence like a doctor on a house call, someone special.

'I just came to tell you how sorry all of us are at Thames Reach.' She reached out and squeezed Amber's arm. 'Phil's specially asked me to give his condolences; and Mary your house head and your form tutor Denise both send their love.'

Love? Amber hardly saw her head of house, while 'Phil' was Philip the new head, Mr P. Green. *Pea Green!* Wouldn't you change it if you were a teacher?

'Thanks.'

'How's your mum?'

'She's all right. She's in bed.'

'Best place. Sleeping pills can help. Anyhow, I don't want to disturb her, and I don't want to disturb you, love. I just want you to know we're thinking about you – and remind you I'm there for you when you come back . . .'

Amber nodded; couldn't find the voice for another thank-you.

'I've got no beef with you being away. There'll be a lot to do, and a lot of support you're going to need to give your mum.' She smiled at Amber. 'We're your family – and I tell you, no bullshit, we're going to look after you.'

'Yeah . . .' Amber snuffled.

And Mrs Feldman left, after giving Amber her mobile number.

Lord above! – a detective, a reporter, and the deputy head – she had some contacts now!

But the contact she wanted most in the world was with the killer who had pushed her Connor off Riverview House.

Chapter Four

Amber had woken to the shock that Connor was dead. He'd been with her in a dream, younger, before he'd had his first skinhead haircut. He was pleased with something she'd given him – it wasn't clear in the dream what it was – but he smothered her with kisses; and she woke, wiping her cheek on the sheet – as the terrible truth hit her. Connor wasn't little any more – and he wasn't any more, any more! He was dead. He'd gone off a balcony of Riverview House and he was all on his own in the next world, with his body left behind and lying in a fridge in the hospital mortuary. Amber shuddered, and she wanted to cry, she had a great need to cry; but again she couldn't. Not even going into Connor's room and kneeling by his bed and praying to him as if he were a saint in heaven could help her to cry.

She definitely didn't care what she looked like for Sunil Dhillon, but she'd have to push past a nose or two on the landing, and she could get caught in a flash for the *Sun* or the *South London Press* – so, yes, she owed it to Connor. She owed it to him to take the trouble –

then he could look down from heaven and feel proud. She re-did her eyes in the bathroom mirror, and made herself late. Debra was hung-over so she took the phone from its base, went out and locked the front door from the outside. Everyone could wait. They'd get no sense out of her mother till later and it saved any hassle.

As it happened, there was no one about: no nosy neighbours and no photographers. She came off the estate and took herself across the traffic-clogged Woolwich Road and up the hill to the Greenwich Observatory: a different person today. Yesterday morning when she'd opened the door to that policeman she'd been a girl doing a rare bunk-off to get tickets at the O_2. Today she was a grown woman who could get straight through on the phone to a man you might soon see on the television; who knew teachers by their first names, and who'd actually had her deputy head standing there in her front room. So she walked, didn't hurry; it was a pull up the hill, but she didn't get out of breath; she made sure she didn't.

Sunil Dhillon was sitting on a park bench, next to a parked Lambretta; no sausage smoke in the air, they hadn't opened yet. He stood as soon as he saw her.

'Yes? What was it you wanted?' she asked him.

'I've got something I want to run past you . . .'

'What's that?' She sat, and he sat, too.

'First off, I want to say he didn't suffer. I've read the report, he died instantly.'

44

'Thank God.' Except, one of her stomach-twisting thoughts was how terrified little Connor would have been, falling: two, three, four seconds of terror on the way down. Did he kick like mad, were his arms going frantic in the air?

'What he was wearing . . .' Sunil went on, '. . . you'd know the clothes – hoody top, jeans, trainers . . .'

'I do.' Probably stuffed in a plastic bag in a mortuary cupboard.

'He had odd laces in his Spivs.'

'So?' Amber frowned – where was this going? 'He was ten. He got up and went out for a climb, or something – he wouldn't care . . .'

'No, I know.' Sunil had put his hands in his coat pockets, as if he was deliberately resisting the temptation to pat hers. Amber looked him in face. He was a good-looking boy, with kind eyes, sleek hair gelled neat, no spikes. 'His left trainer had blue laces, and his right trainer had red.'

'Typical! He wouldn't bother what he tied his trainers with; if a lace broke he'd just get one from someone else.'

'Ah.' Sunil nodded. 'So there's nothing significant about the laces – you don't reckon?'

Amber snorted. 'No, I don't reckon. What could there be *sig-nif-icant* about a pair of laces?' The question hung breathy in the frosty air.

Sunil shrugged. 'It's just that in gang culture – I've

45

read – they use signs like that to show they belong. 'The Blueboyz, or the Barrier Crew – that sort of thing.'

Amber frowned at the cold sun.

'Belts twisted, buckles off-centre, special boot laces, secret tags on walls – signs of membership. Belonging . . .'

'Cobblers!' Amber said. 'My Connor never belonged to anything.' She got up and walked away, past the sausage people who had opened up and were slanting their chalked menu at her. *Not even a proper family* she thought to herself. And she stuck up a finger at them, but it was meant for stupid Sunil Dhillon.

All the same, he had focused her. It was true, what he'd said, because it was true what *she'd* said, originally, and what she believed fervently. Connor hadn't slipped and fallen. Something else had happened with him; and if he hadn't been scared of something and jumped to get out of this life – which her sparky little brother wouldn't do in a million years – what *had* happened? Well, she knew that all right – he'd been harassed or panicked or pushed. But, why? Belonging to a gang meant you were *this* and not *that* – but the little devil hadn't belonged to some gang, that was a load of rubbish. Some of the black kids called themselves the Barrier Crew, but Connor wasn't black – and killing didn't come into it. It was the Edmonton and Walthamstow gangs north of the river that were heavy and tooled up, but it seemed softer in the south. Up off the Old Kent Road there were the Peckham White Boys, and the Brixton lot, who would never dare put a foot in each other's ends unless they wanted a beef; and in the other direction from Thames Reach there were the East-European Romas from Woolwich, and the Charlton Boyz, which was mainly Somali – but no way was little Connor one of them. He lived for climbing. He was his own man.

Sunil Dhillon was well up the wrong tree.

She came to the Woolwich Road – but she didn't cross it to take the side-street that led to the Barrier Estate, she went on along the pavement on the park side, and headed somewhere else, her mind occupied. As her stomach had churned with her grief, all she'd seen in her head up to now was Connor, and the tragedy of it all. But now she concentrated her thoughts on a theory.

He hadn't slipped, and he hadn't been thrown off in some gang warfare. But he had been thrown off by someone! And what she realised now was that all the time at the back of her mind she had this mystery person, some villain on a balcony of Riverview House who had pushed him. Connor's body had been found in the concrete car park – a drop from the ninth floor or the thirteenth, it wouldn't have made much difference which, but the police reckoned he'd been *seen* on the tenth floor – and in Amber's head was the certainty that in one of the flats up there lived the person who had murdered him.

Right. Well, one thing she would do was contact that detective who wore the sort of suit they sold in

Matalan. She'd get in touch with him and find out who'd dished out that *seen* information: because that person needed talking-to about when and exactly where they'd seen Connor; and an answer needed to be given to a vital 'who else was there?' question.

But what sort of thing could have led to anything happening? Had Connor been making someone's life a misery? Was he always up there on the nick, or threatening some old pensioner, or had he met a cat on a climb and got it out of his way, or could he have let someone's precious budgerigar loose?

But, *leading to a murder?*

Or was it more like a mistake, something gone wrong? Was there a person so fed up with Connor's tricks – and Connor could be a right little devil – that he'd held him over the balcony and said, *Next time, son, I'll let you drop!* – and then his hands had slipped. Which would be that other thing, manslaughter.

Amber walked on, bumped into a couple of other pedestrians because her mind was ten floors up in the air. But that was the way her thinking was going. That was the sort of way Connor had died. Been killed. And never mind DC Matalan Man and the BBC's Sunil Dhillon – that was something Amber Long was going to find out herself.

She went to school that afternoon. Thames Reach Academy, all wood and breeze-block. What had happened was that weird thing that comes after the death of a close relative – people are nervous of talking to you, an upside-down sort of fame, and while she'd had texts from her friends, no one had actually phoned, or been round to see her. It was like a taboo, as if they were afraid of saying the wrong thing. So, being Amber, she took it to them, went in during the lunch hour to where they were. And the moment she walked through the school yard, still special, she was instantly besieged. Lauren, Narinder, Oki and Mandy made a whooping run for her to hug her and kiss her and cry with her – actions all standing for words because the right words were hard to find. What can you say to a mate whose brother has died? It's not like a nan or a granddad, however dear they were, however close. Some of them had borne that sadness; but, a little brother dying . . .

Now Amber could cry; her eyes were running black – no mascara she could afford was made for these tears of grief and sympathy. But she didn't care. Her mates were surrounding her, and they walked her like casualty into the building to sort herself in the lavatories, and then to the canteen for a salad and a roll.

'What you come for, Amb? You didn't need to come.'

'It's Holy Joe this afternoon – you've not come for that?'

Amber felt so comforted she almost started crying again. This was what mates were for. With you. On your side. And this was what little loner Connor had never had. No friends' night out at a concert, keeping each others' places; no clubbing at Midnight Express, watching each others' backs.

'No. I just came to tell the office why I'm not coming . . .'

'Everyone knows, Amb. You got given a mench in assembly. You're "in our thoughts", girl!'

'Definitely,' said Lauren. 'We knew you wouldn't have got there so we went down the O$_2$ last night an' ordered our tickets.'

'Lauren's brainwave,' Mandy applauded. 'She's a good'un, eh?'

'Yeah.' Amber nodded. 'She's a good'un. I owe you all.'

'Nah. My treat, this one. Well, my dad's,' Lauren told her. 'He's amadant.'

'Adamant!'

'Anyhow, the sort of dad to have!' Amber said.

And then a silence fell as they all sat round Amber's table while she didn't do more than pick at her salad. The next stage was awkward. They either talked about Connor's death or they didn't talk about it and seemed uncaring. Amber made it easy for them. 'I'm going to the school office. There'll be stuff I've got to do at home, and my mum's useless. Make it my own authorised absence.' And she told them about Dawn Feldman's visit the night before.

'She tell you to come in to school?' Narinder wanted to know.

'No, she was good, paid her respects, told me *not* to come; but that made me not want not coming put down against me . . .'

'Say that again . . .'

Amber smiled. But the feeling she'd had after Dawn Feldman had gone was hard to put into words for this lot. 'You know her, she was good. She made me want to come back even though I can't for a couple of days. So I'm doing it right, getting a mark for the afternoon and going off officially, not just not coming in.' Which, she realised, as the signal for afternoon lessons buzzed through the building, was not a lot clearer than before.

'Right – so you lot clear off, and I'm going to the office. An' I might see you tomorrow.'

Chairs were pushed back with rubber squeals.

'Shall we come round your place?'

'No, not tonight.' Because Amber was a long way off wanting to be cheered up over Connor. She needed to be sad; she wanted to be in mourning. She'd have liked to wear black clothes with a veil over her face like Queen Victoria.

Her mates went one way towards Holy Joe's form room, and she took a left along the corridor towards the school entrance and the office – as a tumble of year seven boys came in the opposite direction. They didn't know her, and somehow she didn't look like a student today, so they gave her a bit more space than

51

normal. They were in school sweatshirts, black trousers, and variations on the no-trainer footwear; talking, laughing, a tangle of arms. As Amber went past them she looked to the floor, didn't want to meet their eyes, no chance of recognition.

And among the shoes she saw something that stopped her where she was. She leant against the wall, looking after them as they went off round a corner.

Because what she had just seen had jumped her heart: the shoe laces on one of those boys, a black kid. Not matching. The left lace blue and the right lace red – *like Connor had worn – according to Sunil Dhillon. And exactly that same way round, left blue and right red.*

She took a deep breath. So was that coincidence – or was it a sign of something? Had Connor been secretly caught up in stuff that was bigger than his own mad, sad way of life?

Then, no! she thought. It was fashion; a craze, like a must-have haircut; the sort of thing schoolkids copy.

Except, Connor never went to school! He wasn't part of anything like that. So *had* he been part of something else, then?

And Amber forgot her authorised absence reason for going in to school, and she headed for the gate, and home.

It wasn't often that the police located Billy Dawson on the first try. When he was tracked down it was usually at the end of a long line of *sorry, guv, just-missed-him*s. But DC Ian Webber struck lucky going to the closed-down cinema in Deptford, where there was no camouflaging Dawson's green S-type Jag parked outside the current venue for the Midnight Express nightclub. Drinks were being unloaded from a cash-and-carry van through a side entrance, while the main doors – painted deep blue in the cheapest of top-coat glosses – were chained closed. So Webber went in at the side, behind a barrow-load of Stella Artois.

He wasn't under-cover. For that he'd be in his baseball cap and trainers, with holed jeans and his distressed leather jacket. This lunchtime he was on an official call, wearing his dark-grey suit like a uniform, might as well have had his number on the lapel. But everything was very polite. He wasn't known to Dawson, he didn't get the 'Mr Webber' treatment given to local CID, instead he was invited to sit on a high stool to talk to the owner across the bar.

'All me licences are in order, an' all me staff are pukka – bar, doors, an' DJs. No illegals – everyone's on the books.'

Denny Benjamin, Dawson's Jamaican minder, came to sit on the stool next to Webber, close. 'Def-in-it. We got 'em all listed in the office.'

'I'm sure.' The DC folded his arms and stared around the room, trained to seem confident however he felt. 'Your personnel's not my problem.'

'Problem? You sayin' there's a *problem*?' Billy Dawson's narrow head sliced its own look around the club. 'You go back to your nick an' talk to your people, officer. Under-age drinkers? Poppers? Hard stuff? Your boys an' girls 'ave been in, we know that – they're the ones who 'ave the extra good time. Ask them an' you'll find out the Midnight Express is as clean as a whistle. Cleaner.' He turned to Denny and laughed, a whiny south London sound. 'You get fluff in whistles – an' there's no fluff in here. Strictly kosher.'

'Kosher,' Denny echoed.

'So, what's your problem? Or are you touching me up for a double scotch on your way to a rotten job?'

'No thanks . . .' Ian Webber leant his elbows on a bar towel . . . 'I just wondered if anyone was giving you any aggravation, opening up here?'

Billy Dawson poured himself a tonic water. 'Like, who? The landlord's happy as a sand boy – "South-east Properties" – I'm a nice little filler while he waits on his planning permission. Can't think of no one else.'

'No one in the nightclub game?'

'Got no opposition round 'ere.'

'No one who supplies you?'

Billy Dawson stood on his toes and spoke over Webber's shoulder to Denny Benjamin. 'Get me them dockets out the office. An' show 'im the wedge in the till.' He focused on the DC. 'That booze you come through the door with – the man's getting cash for that.'

'OK. Fair enough. No other supplier . . . of anything else?'

Billy Dawson leant forward into Ian Webber's face. 'I've told you this is a clean club.'

The DC stared him out. 'Inside, perhaps. No aggravation going on outside – on the streets . . .?'

Billy Dawson straightened up. 'Get your phone out!' he commanded Denny. 'Ring Wolfson. We need a solicitor round 'ere. An' I'll want your ID, son.'

'Certainly.' Webber produced his warrant card, held it up, and recited his police number at Dawson, from memory. There had been no click of a mobile behind him, the minder had tapped in nothing yet. 'When someone dies on the streets we have to talk to a lot of people.'

'Oh, yes. You're only doing your job!'

'So we ask around all the venues . . .'

'An' you think I'm into more than running a nightclub? You think there's some war going on?'

Ian Webber got off the bar stool and walked to the door. 'You said it, Billy – not me.' And he went, but swinging his arms a little self-consciously.

Chapter Five

When Amber got in her mother was moving around the flat as if it were someone else's. She squinted at the kettle like a hung-over party guest trying to work out how to switch it on.

'You're up, then.'

'Just about. Oh, Amber—' She grabbed at Amber and hugged her, smelling of the night.

'Yeah.'

'Silly little devil, doing all that climbing,' she croaked. 'He had to come off, sometime, didn't he?'

Amber disentangled herself. 'No he didn't have to come off! When a ninety-mile-an-hour storm suddenly hits him, OK, perhaps. But not off a balcony of Riverview House on a nice day. Get that idea right out of your head. He never slipped. As for anything else: you tell me, how was he the night before, when he went to bed?'

Debra sat on a kitchen chair, kimono open, breasts shiny with sweat. She stared vacantly up at her daughter.

Amber shook her head. 'You don't know, do you – because you weren't even here! Well, I'll tell you, he was top of the world. I cooked him his favourite tea – egg, sausage and chips – with a couple of Cokes, then we watched an old *Al Murray* on Gold, and he fell about, burping with laughing.' She stared at the sorry sight of her mother. 'He went to bed happy. *Happy!* He never slipped – and he had no reason to jump, neither! That boy was not depressed!'

'What are you saying?' Debra reached for a cigarette.

'Not in the flat!' Amber knocked the packet away.

'So what are you saying?' Debra's ire had cleared her throat like a good cough.

'What I'm saying is, he was pushed! Someone pushed him! Someone up there in Riverview – an' I'm going to go and find out who it was! Someone Connor had done something to, who did something back, and he killed him!'

Feet apart, Debra was leaning on her knees, her head in her hands. 'No,' she said, 'no.'

Amber wanted to get out. Exasperated with this wreck of a woman, she wanted to get to her bedroom and think. With the possibility she'd just put in front of her mother, and the reporter's trainer-laces idea, she'd got stuff to think through, like where to go first: should she talk to that other laces kid at the school, or get up to the tenth floor of Riverview House . . .

'You let me 'ave a fag an' I'll tell you something.' Debra had drawn her kimono around her, and was looking up at Amber with a face that was halfway to being alert.

'What?'

'If you reckon what you reckon, there's something else ties in . . .' She wagged a finger as if she was still drunk.

'I don't get you.'

'Fag!'

Amber slid the packet of Number Six along the kitchen table, while Debra found a disposable lighter in her pocket. She took in a big, first lung-full – and didn't cough. 'You know your dad's in prison . . .'

'I do know.'

'An' you know what 'e's in for . . .'

'Yeah. Half-killing someone.'

'Right.' Another deep drag. 'Well, that wasn't his doing.'

'Oh – he's got a look-alike.'

'He was *made* to do it. Listen . . .' Debra pulled out another chair. 'Sit down for gawd's sake.'

Amber sat.

'He'd run up debts, hadn't he, an' couldn't pay. So whoever it was he owed said he had to do a job for him . . .'

'Cripple someone else who couldn't pay up?'

'You know!'

'No, I'm guessing. But that's what the bullies do in school. Go on, get on with it!' Whatever this was, it was something Amber hadn't known about, although there was always that sort of private stuff where her dad was concerned. She knew he had a name for being hard, but none of that ever came into the house. All the same, her dad having a grudge so big against someone that he'd got five years for sorting him had never really stacked up.

'Then once he was in Marwood I had to give 'im messages on visits. Someone got on to me on the phone. Foreign. Told me Jonny had only paid off half what he owed . . !

'*And?* Amber's head felt strangely light. Where was this going? She'd thought she knew what a rotten family she lived in.

'There was another half he had to pay off – an' according to this bloke he hadn't done it. Something he had to do to someone inside, don't know what it was – but I was told to tell him that he'd live the rest of his life regretting it if he never done it!

'Did what?'

'That's what I don't know! Debra had been dragging so hard on her Number Six that it was finished already. She threw it in the sink and reached again for the packet.

'No!' said Amber – and she shoved the packet into her shoulder bag.

'Gawd!' Debra stood up and held onto the table for support. 'He's got back at Jonny through Connor!' She was shaking. 'He's had Connor killed!'

'*Who?* Who is this "he"?'

'Search me. Where he gambled. Where he owed. Could be bets, could be paying for something he needed . . .'

'You saying drugs?'

'Far as I know he was never serious. An' he couldn't 'ave a drink without falling over. Prob'ly gambling. Poker. The dogs. You know your dad . . .'

Amber frowned. So this was another idea to put into the frame; her mother sounded strong about it and it had the ring of truth; her dad would mourn Connor till the day he died. 'Plenty of stuff to think about,' she said.

And instead of going to her room, she got out of the flat. It was easier to think where there was cleaner air to breathe.

Jonny Long was being paraded in the governor's office again, standing to attention a snap more soldierly this time, eyes-front with a look of respect in them.

'Long . . .' Governor Audrey Simpson read his name off the computer on her desk.

'Yes, ma'am?'

'You will be putting in for a Special Purposes Release for your son's funeral . . .?' Not really a question, Dr Simpson already knew the answer.

'Yes, ma'am.'

Another check with the computer. 'And the date is fixed.'

'Tenth of April, ma'am.'

The governor continued to stare at the monitor. 'And you've been behaving yourself . . . clean cell, punctual to parade, no indiscipline . . .'

'No, ma'am.'

Dr Simpson's eyes came up at Jonny with a hint of *well-you-would-wouldn't you?* 'Good. Then keep it up. You'll be interviewed by a senior officer and if he's satisfied, you'll be notified of the arrangements of your Release on Temporary Licence – a specified number of hours, the escort discreet in suits, but you'll have to be cuffed . . .'

Jonny found a smirk. 'I'm not worried. They'll all know I haven't flown in from Marbella. Ma'am.'

'Otherwise it will be as normal and natural as the occasion demands. But it's a privilege, Long, not a right, and you will not attend any social after-gathering but be returned here immediately following the burial.'

Jonny shifted his weight. 'It's a cremation.'

The governor nodded.

'I'd like to help carry his coffin, ma'am.'

Dr Simpson stared beyond Jonny at the officer who had marched-in the prisoner, a man with a lengthy term of practical experience behind him. He was shaking his head.

'Not possible,' she said. And with a last frown at the computer the governor clicked off Long's screen and nodded at the officer in curt instruction.

'A-bout turn!' And Jonny Long was marched out,

one-two, one-two, one-two – to return to his cell, and not be able to settle to anything for half an hour.

Eventually, 'You ever heard of "Mr P"?' Jonny asked Frank Lodge, his phantom of a cell-mate.

Lodge was sitting upright away from the table, in the hazed light from the window, studying an old *Motor Trader* magazine. He looked up, shook his head, went back to his reading. In fact, Frank Lodge had heard about 'Mr P' many times: Jonny bounced the name off the cell walls frequently, but Lodge was brain-dead to anything except thoughts of the make of vehicle he would use to run down the dealer who'd fooled him.

'You've heard of God, 'aven't you?' Jonny asked.

Lodge didn't even look up.

'Well, that's who he is, Mr P – to tons of mugs like me. He rules our lives. Pulls our strings. One nod of Papendreou's ugly head, an' watch it!'

Lodge turned a page.

'But he's nodded me down once too often now, I tell you – an' one day his game's gonna be stopped . . .'

Lodge's left forefinger kept his place on the page.

'I swear on my boy's mem'ry – 'e's got a total comeuppance to come!'

Frank Lodge looked up, and spoke for the first time in two days. 'You 'ave to get 'em back!'

'You do!'

'You 'ave to get 'em back!'

*

Sunil Dhillon was in the press room at the Boleyn Ground in Green Street, E13, home of West Ham United, waiting for a statement about the manager, who was leaving the club 'by mutual consent'. Sunil was being entrusted to make notes for the local news bulletins, but if the BBC's star football correspondent didn't turn up in the next couple of minutes there was every chance he might front the item himself on national TV. Vicky West was on her way but Sunil's scooter had got through the traffic quicker than her car. Disappointingly for the crowded room the sacked manager wouldn't be there – Luigi Napolitano had already gone home to Italy – but the club's decision to get rid of him needed questioning, because West Ham had similar bad runs of losses most seasons. The rumour was that Napolitano had been seen out clubbing with one of the players' wives, and like all the football hacks in the room, Sunil was rehearsing a polite way of asking a tricky question.

His phone rang. 'Vicky? Where are you?'

'I'm not Vicky – I'm Amber. Amber Long . . .'

'Amber – I'm in a press conference. Can I ring you back?'

'It's about Connor – and what happened to him.'

The door to the club's executive suite opened and a hand came round it, held up and spread out to signify 'five' – five more minutes.

'Own goals,' someone said, which got a small round of applause.

'What did you want, Amber?'

'Could you do me a favour?'

'If I can.' Sunil took another look round at the door through which the first string reporter, Vicky West, would come.

'The police said that the morning Connor died someone was seen on the tenth floor of Riverview House. I need to know who saw that someone, but I don't think the police'll tell me . . .'

'They might.'

'I bet they won't – and I don't want to show myself to be the one wanting to know.'

'So you want me to find out for you?'

'If you could.'

The door to the executive offices opened again – and to groans from the press pack it was only Vicky West who came through it, hunching her shoulders and mouthing, 'Wrong door!'

Sunil waved to her, to show where he and the BBC crew were. He went back to his phone. 'I won't be as long on this as I thought. I'll ring you.'

'Thanks, Sunil. You're a friend.'

'I'd like to think so.'

But already the phone had clicked off.

DC Ian Webber had a message waiting for him in the CID office at Thames Reach police station, asking him to ring the BBC London News reporter Sunil Dhillon, who'd been at the death-by-falling incident. Webber took off his jacket, hung it round the back of his chair, and scratched his head: pantomime for puzzlement. With all the technology available, the request was scribbled on a Post-it note stuck to his desk telephone.

'You take this call?' he asked his female colleague and immediate boss, DS Liz Kwayana.

'While you were out.'

'Been to see Billy Dawson at his Midnight Express nightclub – it's in the old Deptford Globe, stinks of ancient tobacco and new paint.'

'Very literary. And how is our Mister Big?'

'As innocent as you and me: a simple, home-loving nightclub owner who wouldn't know charlie from Chaplin.'

'Huh! So where are you on this boy who fell? What else you got to do?' Liz Kwayana's interest was more than passing: she organised the CID rosters. There would be routine follow-up on the boy's death fall, but unless there were suspicious circumstances to investigate, the CID boss, Detective Superintendent Brewer, wouldn't sanction his people wasting their time following hunches.

'I've got a break-in at Charlton and a flasher who's getting it out on Blackheath.'

'Ha! Must be dedicated! It's good an' cold up there on the Heath.'

'I'll take my magnifying glass. Anyhow, that should

see my shift out – unless something else crops up.' DC Webber looked at the sticky note again, and at his desk telephone. 'Though I've got to say there's something about this kid's death . . . His sister reckons he could never have just fallen, he was too good a climber for that.'

'So no good climbers ever fall? I'll put you through for a word with mountain rescue.'

'Even so . . .'

The sergeant's phone rang, so Webber used his own to call Sunil Dhillon.

'BBC London News.'

'Sunil Dhillon?'

'Speaking.'

'Thames Reach CID; DC Ian Webber. You wanted a word . . .?'

'I did. Thanks for ringing.'

'Yes . . .?'

Down the line the sound of rustling papers could be heard. 'The dead boy's sister – you know, the kid who fell from the block of flats? – she said she was told a boy like Connor was seen on the tenth floor of Riverview House . . .'

'That's what I've got. How can I help, Sunil? Is the BBC doing a piece on this?'

'No! No!' The answer came fast. 'We've done what we're doing, as far as I know. This is something I'm having a little dig at myself.'

'A bit of initiative?'

'Something like that. It's just . . . it would be useful to know . . . who it was who saw a boy on that tenth floor landing. Did the description tally with what Connor Long was wearing? And was the boy the only person who was seen?'

Webber was scribbling some notes. 'Where are you going with this, Sunil? Are you thinking the boy was thrown over and you might have a story?' He blew out his cheeks as he underlined something on his paper.

'I did just wonder – the laces in the trainers; have you looked into the gang element? And his father – Jonny Long, who's in prison – might someone want to be getting at him . . .?'

'We're working through it. We've got a lot on, right now.'

Liz Kwayana heard this and gave DC Webber a look.

'But I'll fetch up the statements on the computer . . .' Which he was already doing, still standing. 'Hang on.' He scanned through two pages on the screen. 'If I give you this, you're not going to get in anyone's way, are you – like ours?'

'More the other way, Ian. It could help you. Amber Long might know if her brother knew the witness – friend or foe . . .'

'Or if they were into anything on the estates . . .?' DC Webber was peering hard at the screen; the Arial font was in a small point. 'Here it is.' Webber clicked to save this page for himself. 'Alfred Walters, number seventy-five Jimmy Seed House – I think it's parallel with Riverview, and they all face east, so if he saw anything from home it'd be from his kitchen or a sitting room at the back.'

'Are you going to give him a look? Interview him again?'

The DC frowned. 'Can't say. But we don't want you or the sister putting mud all over the carpet. Just find out if Amber Long knows the name, that's all.'

'OK.'

'And I might come back to you if there's anything we'd like planted on the news . . .'

'That's fair.'

Webber looked up as Detective Superintendent Brewer walked into the office, no jacket, but a white shirt showing off a silk tie of some rank.

'What's fair, constable?' Brewer was a seasoned London detective, up through the ranks from comprehensive school.

Webber switched off his phone. 'A bit of liaison with the responsible press, guv. About the boy who fell from the flats.' He clicked on 'print'.

The DS took a fresh grip on the folders under his arm. 'No weapon involved, was there – no knife, no firearms?'

'No, sir.'

'Well don't put something into the frame that's not there.'

'No, sir.'

DS Brewer smoothed his oiled hair flat against his head and went on through to push folders in front of other officers: while Webber read what he'd just printed out, the witness statements on the death of a minor, the sparseness of which meant it was either opened-and-closed – or there was a lot yet to be found.

Either way, it had somehow got him hooked.

Chapter Six

No two floors of Jimmy Seed House were the same. Some had like-minded residents who took communal care to keep the place pleasant – mats at the front doors and flowerpots on the window-sills. Some were homes to scrap collections of one-wheeled kids' bikes and wonky scooters. Some were dog-fouled, and on the second floor there was a door with a notice stuck behind its crinkly glass reading: *YOU BETTER HAVE A BLOODY GOOD REASON FOR NOCKING HERE.* But most landings housed a mixture of residents as individual and as different as those down any street. The seventh floor of Jimmy Seed House was one of those: five different flats – a pushchair outside one, a 'post-horn' mail box outside another, the rest unremarkable – each opening onto the balcony with its blue toughened-glass balustrade, low enough to see over but high enough to prevent accidents.

To get through the security door at the block's main entrance Amber tapped in a random flat number, and when someone squawked an answer, her friend Lauren said, 'Parcel!', and the door gave.

Amber was pleased Lauren had come. In defiance of being told not to go round Lauren had buzzed Amber's flat, anyway. Debra was out – she'd pulled herself together and gone to work shelf-filling and queue-busting at Asda. Together with her child benefit it was where the Longs' money came from; and Connor's part of that would soon be stopped. But Amber reckoned the real reason Debra went to work was for the sympathy; she'd have them all over her with hugs and kisses and cuddles.

Lauren was a good mate; she'd helped sort the kitchen before they made themselves a couple of ham rolls. A tall, blonde girl, pretty in a gauzy sort of way – where Amber could have played *Carmen* – the two of them hit it off well, opposites attracting. Lauren lived in a fancy-brickwork-and-decking town house looking onto the river, with a musician dad and a midwife mum – who were determined their daughter would go to the local school and mix with the rest of Thames Reach.

'You want to come round my place? See a movie?' Lauren had an HD television the shape and size of a door on its side.

'Not tonight, Lor. There's something I've got on.'

'Stuff about – ?'

'Connor, no. Well, yes it is, but not . . . official . . . stuff.' And Amber had told Lauren what it was: that if Connor had been seen on the tenth floor of Riverview House, she wanted to meet this last person who'd seen him alive.

71

'Yeah, I'd want to do that, too. I'll come with you if you like – just in case it's an old perv.'

Now the two of them were coming up to the seventh landing.

'How . . . do you know . . . the name and address?' Said between grabs of breath: up the stairs because the lift stank.

'This reporter . . . BBC . . . Sunil Dhillon – he's a trainee on the London news.' Amber stopped and steadied her lungs. 'The one who borrowed Connor's picture.' But for a reason she didn't know, she kept their Greenwich Park meeting to herself. 'He found out for me.'

'What number?' They were on the landing now, walking past the pushchair outside seventy-one.

'Seventy-five.'

'That's four along.'

'Lor, I *am* glad you came!' And they both giggled, but more from nerves than wit.

They walked along the landing until they stopped just short of number seventy-five, where Amber stood and 'read' the door, to get some idea of the man who lived inside. Was the paintwork clean, wiped down where the hands always went? – yes, it was. What else? It still had the small original letter box – unlike Amber's door – so whoever lived here wasn't a catalogue freak with packets being delivered all the time. The door was fitted with a Chubb lock and a spy-hole; but there were none of the personal touches people add when they can afford them. An ordinary place.

Amber's heart was starting to race as the moment came: not so much from nerves about who would answer the door, but about what the man had seen. Might he have seen Connor slip or fall, or deliberately throw himself off? None of these things were possibles in Amber's mind, but sometimes the impossible *was* possible, wasn't it? Even older, loving sisters could be mistaken about what went on in their brothers' heads. Or might this Alfred Walters sound as if he was lying? And if he was, why would he? Could what Debra said be true – that some revenge had gone on from the prison, some terrible punishment dished out – and this man living here was part of a cover-up?

'Be interesting to know if this bloke's ever been inside,' she hissed at Lauren.

'Why?'

Amber preferred not to answer. There was a bell push on the door, a leftover from before the squawk box entries were added downstairs. She pushed it, it still worked, but instead of a rasping unwind on the other side of the woodwork what they heard were the chimes of *You'll Never Walk Alone*. And sure enough, it was a "Scouser" who opened the door to them: a small elderly man in bright red glasses who stared from one to the other.

"As me luck changed? Did I die an' I'm up in 'eavun?"

He looked out along the landing. 'Or uv I won a competition?'

'Depends if you went in for one,' Lauren told him, zipping up her jacket.

'Come through, anyhow, whorever you want – don' like conduct'n me affairs out here.' He was dapper, in black silk shirt and black chinos, what hair he had gelled along the sides of his head with enough sheen to show Amber a glint of her reflection. They went in. Well, they were two and he was one – and he seemed twinkly and harmless. He took them into his sitting room at the back, which was not at all what Amber had pictured from the ordinary look of his front door. The furniture was all soft black leather, the carpet the grey sort they had in offices; and prominent around the walls were caricatures of Liverpool footballers, a couple of actors, and the prime minister, all on that A3 paper the street artists use in Leicester Square. Along under the window in the best of the light was a wide table with pens, brushes, inks, paper and paints, like a studio set-up – and an unfinished watercolour of a lake and mountains.

'What c'n I do for you two? You 'aven't come to be done?' Mr Walters waved them to sit on the low-backed three-seater. Amber shook her head, looked at his shoes, which were as shiny as his gel, neat feet like a dancer's.

She came straight to it: this dude was into fleecing

tourists up west, not sorting prison disputes, she was sure of that. 'My brother. He died two days ago. Went off the tenth floor of Riverview House . . .'

'Yours! Aah. Poor kidda. I saw 'im.' He turned to look towards the parallel block.

'Fall? You saw him fall?' Amber couldn't ask this sitting down: she stood, staring through the un-curtained window across the space, then fiercely into the man's eyes.

'Ca'm it, love. I saw 'im twice – down there, on the ground, and over there, on the balcony. Opposite way round o'cose: balcony, then on the ground, later . . .'

'The same boy?' Lauren got up to ask.

'Same clobber – looked like the same laddie to me.'

'. . . Only you do wear glasses . . .' she went on.

'Fair enough. Fair comment.' Alfred Walters was elderly, yes, but definitely no old dodderer. Amber turned to Lauren to give her a look to take it easy. 'Close up, I need the specs – but distance is A-One. An' I'm used to tekin' in detail.' He waved an arm around the walls. 'I c'n cert'nly tell a kid in a grey hoodie from a lass in red wi' a basket o' cakes, skippin' to her nanna's . . .' He looked at Lauren and winked, his face dead straight otherwise.

'And the boy you saw in the hoodie – who everyone's taking as being my brother – what was he doing when you saw him on the balcony?' This was what Amber desperately needed to know. 'Was he going up the building, wall climbing, that sort of thing?'

Alfred Walters took off his glasses to stare at Amber. 'Din't they tell you, girl? 'E was runn'n. When I saw 'im the lad was runn'n, along from the stairs end, over ther', plain as daylight.'

'Where? Where was he running *to*?'

'One o' the flats further along? Had to be, else it's a dead end! Din't take a lot o' notice. I was do'n a commission. Looked up, saw 'im, typical kid muck'n-about – went back to me board. 'Eard the buvver later, an' see 'im down on the deck. God rest 'im . . .'

Amber looked round at Lauren, whose face said she believed all of this – which went for Amber as well: unless this guy was a brilliant actor. 'OK, thanks,' she said.

'When I saw 'im down there I phoned the p'lice – told 'em wha' I'd seen.'

Amber nodded, found a smile and made for the door – but suddenly stopped. 'There's different sorts of running, though, isn't there? There's jogging; there's being late and got to catch a bus; and then there's running like hell because you're being chased . . .'

'Tha's the one!' Alfred Walters' red glasses were still up on top of his head. 'If tha's wha' you're ask'n me?'

'It is!'

'Like someone wor after 'im – now I think about it. Sprinting like a grey'ound, 'e was. Then that's kids' stuff, in't it? Chasin' abou' the place? Natural.'

'No!' Amber said. 'Not always.' And with a polite thank-you to the caricature king, the girls went, dropping down the flights of stairs without a word to one another, while through Amber's head the questions were running. Did she go to Sunil Dhillon, did she go to Matalan Man, did she tell her mum – or did she wait until she'd done a certain something else she wanted to do? Something that might give her a bit more to go on . . .?

When Amber went in to Thames Reach Academy next morning Dawn Feldman was just inside the school gate. As soon as she spotted Amber her face flowered in a smile. 'All right?' she asked. 'How's it going, Amber?'
   'Not so bad.'
Amber had got up early enough to iron a black blouse and sharpen a pleat in her skirt. The night before she'd washed her hair and pulled out her school bag, which still had the books in it from three days before, when Connor was still alive. Not that she'd come in today for the education: her eyes wouldn't be on any books or whiteboards – they'd be on boots and shoes, and laces: because she wanted to find that kid with the blue and the red she'd seen before, and ask him a couple of crucial questions.
   'Glad you came in. And I think – I *think* – I've got your tutor group this morning.'
   Amber frowned. Mrs Feldman hadn't been on her timetable before.

'Innovation and change. Down as "Liberal Studies" – going to use it for anything, off curriculum. A bit of elbow room, some real education . . .' She was gleaming; Dawn Feldman could spread enthusiasm with her eyes.

'Sounds good.' But Amber wasn't sure how long she'd be staying.

Lauren came in through the gate, and Mandy, with high-fives and hugs.

'Hiya, you two. I'll see you later, ask Amber, she knows.' And the deputy head went off to sort a dispute about a broken iPod.

'Monitor! You'll be head girl next, Amb!'

Amber looked at her friends. 'I'll never be a girl again,' she said quietly, 'head or otherwise.' And that truly was the way she felt; today she was wearing suitable clothes for school like fancy dress. But she also knew she couldn't just patrol the corridors with her eyes on people's feet, she had to search for that laces boy in the normal course of events. When she found him, she'd back him into a corner and get some answers out of him – or she might find out his name and do a bit of snooping round his place. That was one question she was asking: were he and Connor in some gang together? And was there some gang enemy they both had? And the other question she was going to ask would be put to Debra. When she got home, when her mother was back from wherever she went after her

78

Asda shift, she was going to have a long talk with her about those prison threats she'd been told to pass on. There was a hell of a lot of stuff to do right now . . .

Dawn Feldman got them hooked. She walked into the form room, tripped on a loose floor-block and swore. *'Shit!'* That sat them up. 'Argument!' she said. 'Do you buy the *Big Issue*?' she asked Charlie Imeson.

'I sell it, Miss!'

'"Mrs Feldman", if you don't mind. But you don't really sell the *Big Issue*, do you?'

'No, Miss.'

'Ever bought it?' One or two had. 'Ever given money to those rough sleepers who sit in doorways, or next to cash machines?' Again, a few had. 'Anyone here always refuses to give money . . .?' A lot did. 'Why? Why give? Why not give?' And the debate opened up. From a cold, reluctant class Dawn Feldman dragged out all sorts of reasons for not giving – beggars should go and get jobs, they only want money for drugs, the government should provide for them, most of them are immigrants and ought to go back and beg in their own countries. But others thought there wasn't enough cheap housing around, people in the gutter needed a leg up, and Mark Granger said, 'If you split with your family an' run off from home, you've still got to eat, haven't you?'

'You know someone's done that?'

'Me. Then I went home for a curry.'

79

But the way Mrs Feldman was listening to him, no one laughed. On Saturday mornings she held councillor surgeries for young people like him. She switched on the computer and up on the whiteboard came two pages of text. It was an excerpt from *Out on the Cutting Edge* by Lawrence Block.

'Look at that,' she said; 'Lawrence Block has taken both sides of the argument, from the mouth of one character, Matt, and from a friend of his called Eddie.'

Amber read it: this was the sort of stuff they'd been saying, for and against giving to beggars. *'You gotta be the softest touch on the whole West Side. What are you, Matt, just a boy who can't say no?'* The against had some good points, quite persuasive – although the last words were from Matt. *'I give away a few bucks every day, that's all. It doesn't hurt me and it doesn't help anybody very much. It's just what I do these days.'*

'A way of life, an attitude to life,' Dawn Feldman said. 'Argument, and attitude, that's what's all around us, and what we see in films and plays and what we read in books – from Shakespeare to Malorie Blackman. And the great thing is, you don't have to agree with any of it. It makes you think, you get focused – and please God you get entertained along the way.' She emphasised it. *'Pleasure,* my friends.'

'As much as Half Past Yesterday?' Lauren asked.

'Just as much! Because *you* can talk about Si's singing, Lor, while I can argue for his keyboard.'

Strewth! thought Amber.

'And before you lot think I'm a fan, I read all about Half Past Yesterday in a review. I *read* it!'

His singing, definitely his singing, Amber thought to herself. Meanwhile, Mrs Feldman hadn't taken a breath before she was telling them that for follow-up – 'if any of you want to do it – and it won't bring me out in a sweat either way' – they could watch a film, any film, their choice, and pick out a scene where two people take different stands – then decide which one of them has the winning argument, and why. 'And ask ourselves, does the same stuff happen in real life?'

'My dad had a shoot-out with his brother!' Peter Hajdu called out. 'Is the fastest gun wins.'

'You could look at a few westerns, too.'

Eventually they all piled out of the form room, Dawn Feldman beating Mark to the door with a long arm across him. And as Amber hit the corridor she suddenly realised that she was looking up and about her – not at the floor. Just for forty minutes she'd forgotten about laces, and her troubles.

Chapter Seven

He wasn't there. She wished she'd taken more notice of the laces kid when she'd seen him before – because if he was in the school today he had to be hiding in the lavatories. Every pair of shoes she looked at was either Velcro-strapped or done up with regular black laces; coming in to Thames Reach Academy had been a waste of time on the Connor front. It was good to have the comfort of her mates around her, and she'd enjoyed the session with Dawn Feldman – but Amber's real business these days was not her education. It was finding out who had killed her brother. Alf the Artist had told them that Connor was being chased along that landing. The boy had been running for his life! *But running away from whom?* That was the million dollar question! Now – standing in a cubicle in the lavatories where she could be on her own for five minutes – her mind went to that other possibility her mother had talked about, the prison revenge. Debra had been phoned and given warnings to pass on to Jonny Long – which meant that Amber's dad was meant to do something on top of the GBH that had put him in prison. To pay off what he owed someone, he had to do more than put one baggage handler in hospital; he had to hurt someone in Marwood. So the next big question was, had he done the business, or not? If he'd done it, he'd paid his debt – and Connor's death wasn't down to revenge. Well, there was only one way to find out: she would do what she hadn't intended doing – she'd go to Marwood with Debra on visiting day. She really didn't want to be in that grief of talking about the funeral – but she would go with her mother, and she'd ask her dad, straight out. She'd ask him if some sort of revenge attack could have killed Connor – or had her dad done what he'd been told to do?

And if he hadn't, the next question would be, *who?* Who was the monster who would kill a kid to get back at a grown man? Knowing that would be the first step towards taking her own revenge.

The next visiting day at HMP Marwood was on the Friday. Debra sometimes went on one of the two visits permitted each month, but mostly she didn't: her clubs-and-pubs lifestyle with Winston and his friends didn't leave room for much more than getting to work each day. Besides, prison visits needed organising and she was never organised enough to ring the prison visits number so that Jonny could fill out a visiting order; and then she had to remember to take her ID with her; which she'd forgotten more than once. But Amber had seen a slight change in her mother since Connor's death. Winston didn't seem to be on the scene any more, and she kept talking about wanting to 'find out what all them phone calls meant'. So Amber was going on the visit this time – to put her own questions to her father. And if something half useful came out of his slack mouth she'd start making plans of her own.

The train got in on time, the Marwood bus from the town quickly filled up with women and a couple of children, and within two hours of leaving home Amber and her mother were showing their IDs at the main gate and being checked through to the visitors' centre.

Amber always wanted to snort at this place: with its prison-made toys and 'Marwood' mugs on sale, a 'Friends' help desk, a play area, toilets, baby-change, and 'screws' with smiles, it was like school on an open evening when you never hear a teacher raise their voice above a smarm. Amber had brought her student card for ID, and Debra had remembered her child benefits book. Going on in, they put their cash, keys and bags in one of the lockers, stepped through the metal detector and were rub-down searched by a woman smelling of spearmint, who then looked in their mouths for drugs; and when they'd had their hands marked with an ultraviolet stamp they were allowed into the visiting hall, to sit at a table and wait for Jonny Long.

'Let me do the talking,' Debra said. 'Funeral first.'

Which had her rooting in her pockets for the first tissue of the afternoon.

That word hit Amber, too; just the fact of it being said between them. 'Take a deep breath. Think of Dad – he won't want to crack up in here.'

'Yeah . . .'

And suddenly Amber's head went light and her heart thumped as there he was – shown in through the door from the cell-blocks by a pimply prison officer who looked about ten. Her dad! Thin before, and thinner now, but smart in a white shirt and jeans, his hair done differently, somehow. The stupid man who could have had his boy killed for something he'd failed to do himself; but who had to be grieving worse even than Debra; because they'd been a pair, him and Connor . . . That was how mixed-up it all was.

"Lo.' Her dad pulled out a chair on the other side of the table, after leaning across for a quick touch of foreheads with Debra, and a peck on the cheek for Amber. Probably not allowed, Amber thought – except, they must know in here – he's lost his little boy.

'How you doin'?' Debra sat, her hands on the table in full view like a veteran visitor.

'I'm gutted.'

'I've got the date.' There was no doubting what date she meant.

'I know it. They reckon I can come. Just for the service.'

'Greengates Crem.', Debra said. 'Ten a.m.'

Jonny Long looked down at his chewed nails, up at Amber. 'But they won' let me help carry the coffin . . .' His eyes welled up, and Amber's threatened to spill, so she took the talk in that other direction.

'Do you still owe someone?' she asked. 'Someone with muscle?'

'Nah. Stopped smoking, don't do drugs – pay my way on the canteen . . .'

'I don't mean in here, necessarily.' Amber leant forward, came to the crux as Debra started shaking her head. 'Mum said you had threats. Something you had to do for someone . . .'

'I done it, babe, didn't I?' And his face had that same innocent-but-guilty look that Connor used to have – only this wasn't about taking the last can of Coke.

'Yeah, we know you did. Five years' worth. But you had more warnings after all that. While you've been inside. Mum took 'em, off the phone. They said you had to do something to someone in here, or else!' Amber stared into her father's eyes, and he held her gaze – till he broke contact and went back to looking at his hands. 'And when you didn't do it . . .' she went on, husking it from her throat. ' . . . when you didn't do it after the second warning . . .' She could hardly say it.

'Wha'?'

'That's when they went an' killed Connor. One theory. They . . . killed . . . your . . . boy!' Her face was five centimetres from her father's, she could smell prison chips on his breath. 'He was seen being chased along the landing just before he went over.'

'No contact, young lady. Sorry.' A burly prison officer had come across from leaning against the nearest wall.

Amber sat back. Her father didn't acknowledge the PO but went on staring into Amber's face, mouth shut tight.

'So – who was it? Who do you owe that much? We're talking your own kid's life?' She had to say it: cruel though it was, she had to say it, because that was why she'd come. *And because what had happened had been cruel to more people than Jonny Stupid Long.*

'I'll deal with it! I'll sort it!' her father croaked. 'I will deal! OK?' And suddenly he pushed back his chair, got to his feet, and walked between the tables to the door. Visit ended. Without a goodbye, and without Amber getting an answer to *who?*

Sunil Dhillon sat on the press benches of Stone Marsh Crown Court. Sitting in a modern building near the river north of Dartford, the court was hearing the case of a cocaine consignment intercepted on its way into the capital – with a street value running into millions of pounds. Being southeast of London this was local news, but the quantity of cocaine involved meant it would make the national bulletins. As well as Dermot Mark, the BBC's number one crime correspondent Emmanuel

Glinsberg was there, leaving Sunil with little more to do than keep the others' seats warm every time they left the courtroom to do their updates, making notes of everything said while Glinsberg and Mark were outside, being famous.

But the case interested Sunil. Much of what he was shadowing as a trainee reporter with the BBC was to do with crime – which was a lot more interesting than commuter problems or council recycling targets. And this drugs bust had the makings of a good story when it all came out.

For the Crown, the prosecuting counsel had outlined how the operation worked, which although clever was very straightforward. The illicit drugs came into Britain at the Thames Europort container dock at Dartford, hidden in cargoes of strong-smelling spices like cardamom and saffron, which were intended for the Asian and Arab restaurant trades. These drugs consignments were regularly pulled out at Dartford by a Europort worker, then packed into the large boot of an old BMW ready to drive them round the M25 then into London, or up the A2 and through the Blackwall Tunnel – any route that avoided the congestion charge cameras. The trail was lost in London, the drugs presumably delivered to whoever was going to package it into street-size portions. But without its destination this was where the prosecution case faltered – and why instead of the Mr Big in the dock all they'd got was this courier, a small blue-chinned man called Andrei Basescu. Basescu lived in Gravesend, and while the police might guess at the name of his drugs boss they couldn't say it without any proof. And Basescu stayed loyal, wouldn't make a statement of any sort – settled for a very long prison sentence rather than one day face up to his Mr Big.

But the way Basescu had been caught was gripping all the same; where Sunil could see a glimpse of clashing gangs, because whoever had tipped-off Revenue and Customs had wanted him caught – and that wouldn't be his own people. The grass had to be working for someone else, who used some other port of entry – otherwise it would be fouling their own doorstep to eliminate the Dartford competition. The tip-off led to a police road-block being thrown across the A2 near the Bexley turn-off, where the fifty mph limit slowed everything down. Just before the slip-road ran south into Bexley village, Basescu's BMW had been pulled over into a hotel car park and its boot opened up, and there it was – neat, tight, and in tens of kilos: thousands of pounds worth of cocaine, packaged up as cardamom spice.

With Mr Big identified or not, it had been a huge quantity of drugs for the police to keep off the streets of London. And now, with Basescu refusing to enter a plea of either guilty or not guilty, everyone waited to see how long the man would serve in prison.

Now, the moment had come: and it was for what happened next that reporters wait. After Basescu had been found guilty, before sentence was passed he was asked if there was anything he wanted to say. In very clear language the judge told him that giving the name of the man who paid him would cut his sentence by years. And Basescu did wish to say something. The court went quiet. Sunil Dhillon had his pencil ready.

'Răz!' Basescu shouted in a strong accent, spitting on the floor of the dock – contempt for which two years was tacked on to his long sentence. And which sent Glinsberg off out to his live bulletin, fishing for his mobile phone to ring round underworld contacts who might know the 'Răz' Basescu meant, who had to be big in the drugs world.

Chapter Eight

Amber hardly slept at all. The evening before Connor's funeral she'd been with Debra to the Co-op chapel-of-rest to say her last goodbye, trying to come to terms with it by telling herself that this calm, still, beautiful little face wasn't Connor any more – it was only the mask he'd worn for his ten years in this rotten world. Debra had kissed him on the forehead but Amber had just stood looking at him through blurred eyes. *So, where was the real Connor now?* Was he in heaven with Jesus, cracking jokes and nicking the last nectar – or was he burning in hell for doing all sorts of bad stuff she didn't know about? And did she believe in all that religious talk, anyway? Wasn't it more likely that Connor Long had just been here in Thames Reach for a bit, eaten a few meals, played a few tricks, romped a few romps, climbed onto a few roofs, and gone: curtain closed, door shut? Did she really think she would see him again one day – and would he even recognise her if he was still ten and she was an old woman of ninety when she died? Would he still jump on her back and ride her round the room the way he used to? Grief kept Amber awake –

picturing that lonely little body waiting to be cremated: because the funeral was going to be the end of Connor as he was. His looks, his 'tin ribs', his tickly underarms and his size-six feet were all going to be incinerated down to the bones, to ashes. And there would be nothing left of him except photographs to look at. Ever. For billions of years until the end of time, Connor would not exist. Which was the last thought she had, her pillow wet and her throat too full to swallow, before she finally went off to sleep, minutes before her alarm clock rang.

And then it was the whiff of brandy for Debra's breakfast, 'just to hold me together', and the most painful getting-ready of all – dressing for a funeral. Amber had chosen a knee-length plain black dress, which she would cheer up with a gold-coloured brooch Connor had once given her. Debra had gone for a black trouser suit which would 'do all day' – by which she meant back at the Captain Cook down by the river afterwards, where there'd be a few sandwiches on the bar, and a glass of sherry. Neither of them had run to new coats, though, and it being a chilly April day, Amber would wear her parka, and Debra her fake fur. A big deal for Amber was doing her face and hair. She'd shampooed herself shiny the night before, and her make-up was going to be real 'film star' for her Connor.

She'd kept her red roses in water overnight; now they were tied ready, with kitchen roll drying the stalks. Her mother had ordered the family wreath from the florist in the market – a football motif, when Connor had never played football in his life. And suddenly, like that, still getting themselves together and almost an hour before the hearse was due, a buzz came from the entry. It was two aunts – Debra's older sisters – when everyone had been told to go direct to the crematorium; but they were a god-send really because that meant it had started, it wasn't just Amber and her mother; now they were in the hands of what was going to happen.

She thought she wouldn't breathe again when someone said the hearse had arrived; and when she braved herself to look, there it was down in the parking, a shiny hearse with a wreath on top – which wasn't their floral football – with a few neighbours standing about.

At the sight of the hearse Debra caught her breath, too, the back of her hand to her mouth; she had to be helped away from the balcony's edge. 'Oh, my good God!' Below them the man in black stood erect, top hat on his head, both gloves held in one hand as he looked up.

'Coming!' Auntie Pat called down, while her sister Paula took the door key from Debra's fingers and locked up the flat.

Amber's head reeled as she stared down; her legs went to water. Clutching her roses, which pricked without her feeling a thing, she leant against the locked door.

'Big breaths, Amb. Come on, girl. Us Smiths c'n do what we've got to do . . .' Auntie Paula eased her away from the door and led her behind Auntie Pat and Debra towards the lift. Down they went, jolting a bit at the bottom, coming out to a ground-level view of the hearse and the limo lined up behind it. By now Amber was doing this only for Connor. She wanted to curl up on the ground and never move again; but for Connor she held her head high and followed her stooped mother towards the hearse. So small! The coffin was so small! Ten years of life in a polished box that would have fitted across their hearth. And as if it were glass, all she could see was that little kid inside, all alone. He'd always been a loner. They'd had their romps and laughs together, him and his dad had mucked about like two kids; but deep down he'd always been Connor with his own stuff going on. Well, he was a loner now, all right. On the coffin was the floral football – so whose was the wreath on the roof of the hearse? The aunts'? Her dad's, from prison? It was big, expensive, beautifully arranged from irises and daffodils – and the colours were the clue, blue and yellow. Even before she read its card she knew it was from Thames Reach Academy. *In memory of Connor Long, a student-to-be of TRA.* Mrs Feldman! Dawn Feldman had done this, Amber knew; been true to her word, and supportive . . .

The door of the limousine was held open for them: Debra first, then the sisters, three across the back – and

Amber on the little seat that pulled down. Click, the door was shut quietly, and with the man in the top hat leading the way, Connor Long's small funeral procession went at walking pace out of the Bartram House parking and onto the main road, where people stopped, looked, and some made sympathetic nods at the size of the coffin. One old man removed his cap and stood to attention as the cortege went past; and then the funeral director in the top hat got into the hearse and the whole thing speeded up – to get to the crematorium on time.

Jonny Long was in a prison car wearing a dark grey suit, handcuffed to a tall prison officer in a blazer and fawn trousers. So much for discretion: he'd stand out like a parrot among pigeons. They were early at the crematorium, waiting in the back of the car while the driver – the other escorting officer – played Pop Gold FM on the radio. Such sensitivity. Across the car park a knot of people stood outside the waiting room to chapel 'A' – presumably neighbours and friends, all ages – some smoking, all wearing brave little smiles.

'God, my guts!' Jonny Long said. 'D'you reckon there's a lav in that waiting room?'

The driver looked round. 'You were s'posed to go before we left.'

'I did. An' I wanna go again.'

The two prison officers exchanged looks. 'You're not having these cuffs off!' Blazer told him. 'I'm used to prisoners' stink – if you want to go I'll be in there with you, tight as you like.'

'He's got a nose like a blocked chimney,' the driver said.

'Cheers!' Jonny looked from one to the other. 'But it's passing over.' And he slumped back in his seat with the same look on his face Connor always had when he didn't get what he wanted.

The hearse glided in at walking pace, and the first person Amber saw was her father. Jonny Long was sitting in the back of a black car, looking out of it with a face like a lost kid. Hard? How did that man have a reputation for being hard? Pathetic was the word. The driver of the prison car was opening its rear door – and out he got, smart in a suit, handcuffed to a geek of a man in holiday clothes – and with his free hand he waved at her and Debra. Their car drew up behind the hearse, and out they got, too, Debra calmer now and holding herself together after another swig of Dutch courage in the car. And Amber's face lit up a fraction when she saw who was in the group of people standing outside the chapel – Lauren, Narinder, Oki and Mandy – all good mates, all out of school and dressed with respect in black. She waved, and mouthed them a kiss. Apart from that, everyone's eyes were on the coffin.

In a group with Debra and the aunts, Amber was ushered towards the door, the chapel organ playing

'Amazing Grace'. And suddenly standing there behind them was her dad.

'All right, Debs?'

'Yeah.'

'Amb?'

'Yeah, I'm all right. I'll be all right.'

'We all will be – later.'

And in they went, to the first pew on the right – the aunts against the oak panelling, then the prison officer and Jonny Long, then Debra, with Amber on the aisle end – and no attempt made to hide her dad's handcuffs: well, everyone knew, didn't they? But what did he mean by what he'd just said?

Behind them came the others – the friends, a couple of neighbours, two women from Asda, and the relatives from further afield – until the chapel was half-filled. Some sat down straight away, others first bowed their heads to the front. Someone knelt to pray, and had to be helped up afterwards. Now the funeral director, without his top hat, walked to the front of the chapel and gestured for everyone to stand as the vicar came up the aisle, leading the procession.

'I am the resurrection and the life, saith the Lord: he that believeth in me, though he were dead, yet shall he live; and whosoever liveth and believeth in me, shall never die.'

The organ started a funeral march, and the slow creak of boots said that the coffin was following.

Everyone turned to watch its short journey, Amber with her breath held, the posy ready; and as the coffin came level with her – little Connor in there, near enough to touch – she put it on the coffin's top, steadied and centred by a bearer. Her eyes welled as the coffin was placed on the plinth and the men came away, leaving Connor up there, all on his own again.

The vicar stood behind the lectern. 'We brought nothing into this world, and it is certain we can carry nothing out.' He paused, because two metres away Amber's dad was making noises in his throat, fidgeting his arms and the handcuffs. The vicar nodded at him, understanding the man's grief. 'The Lord gave, and the Lord hath taken away; blessed be the name of the Lord.'

And as Amber stared, her eyes suddenly widened, cleared, dried instantly: because never mind her father getting agitated, what was that she'd seen, looking round to put her posy on Connor's coffin? What had caught her eye as she'd lowered her head? *A pair of trainers! A pair of grey trainers with laces, the left lace blue and the right lace red over on the other side of the aisle!*

'Please sit.'

Amber sat. Jonny Long had to be pulled down.

'The Lord is my shepherd: therefore can I lack nothing...'

But Amber didn't want to sit – she wanted to stay standing so she could see who was wearing those laces, but to look round again would be too obvious: everyone would see where she was looking; so she stuck it out – her neck starting to quiver with her effort to stay still while the vicar read from the Bible. As he closed it Jonny Long had tried to get up again, but the men on each side of him pulled him down. And with another nod at him, the vicar took off his glasses, leant on the lectern, and went into what was supposed to be a comforting speech, which got personal about Connor and the Longs, trying to give some sort of hope – where, for Amber, there was none to be had. Her father was straining along the pew and her mother was shaking; but never mind all this false hope, all she wanted right now was to get a good look at whoever was wearing those laces. That was the real future.

Her chance came as they stood for a hymn, the organ accompanied by croaks and whines; no one at all in the mood for singing – Jonny Long least of all, facing the ceiling and nodding as if he were counting.

> 'The King of love my shepherd is,
> Whose goodness faileth never;
> I nothing lack if I am His,
> And He is mine for–ever . . .'

Now Amber took a look over her shoulder, starting at the rear of the chapel so it wouldn't seem as if she was targeting anyone. And there was her second surprise – because she knew those two men in the back row, not standing together, but not too far apart. One was Sunil Dhillon, the TV reporter; and the other was Matalan Man from the local police, neither of them up for singing, either. And with her eyes scanning up the aisle she shot a quick look across at the person wearing those trainer laces. It was a black kid in a leather bomber over a blue PlayCo sweatshirt, about her own age – but not anyone she recognised from her school, and definitely not the year seven school kid she'd seen in blue and red laces before. And he was standing silent and staring sideways at someone on Amber's side of the aisle: just staring, like someone refusing to blink first.

'Perverse and foolish oft I strayed,
But yet in love he sought me,
And on his shoulder gently laid,
And home rejoicing brought me . . .'

Her dad was whining in his throat, nowhere near the tune, as Amber ricked her neck twisting to get a look at that someone on her side of the chapel. It was a kid about eighteen or nineteen with rough hair and a face as pale as the hymn sheet. And he was doing what the laces kid was doing – just staring back across the aisle with a defiant look on his face.

And so through all the length of days
Thy goodness faileth never:
Good shepherd may I sing thy praise
Within thy house for ever.'

So what was all that about? *Had* Connor been part of some gang, like the reporter thought? The two laces kids she'd seen were black, like members of the Barrier Crew, and Connor was white: but she wasn't an expert – and he had worn the same laces. Was there stuff going on she needed to find out about? Was that why the reporter and the policeman were there at the back of the chapel?

Her father barked a loud cough like a dog, and she pulled herself away from those thoughts. *Later!* Right now she was here for her Connor, she was saying goodbye to her brother – everything else could wait. Next to her, Debra was in a real state – because after the hymn the vicar began reading out some of the stuff Amber had written about Connor around the house: that his favourite food was sausage and chips, his bits of kindness like the birthday card he made for the old man next door, the trick he played on him with glue on the doorknob, and the sound of his laugh that had everyone laughing. Which would never be heard again in Bartram House.

Debra nearly went; and the prison officers were having a hard time restraining her dad; while Amber tried to force herself to feel the same hopelessness, go where they were – but she couldn't. She still couldn't get those laces out of her head, and those hateful stares across the chapel.

'Most merciful Father, who hast been pleased to take unto thyself the soul of this thy child; Grant to us that we may be joined hereafter with thy blessed saints in glory everlasting; through Jesus Christ our Lord. Amen.'

Everyone had been praying – except Amber, but whose gaze suddenly shot to the front – because as the praying went on, Connor's coffin was slowly on the move. And so was her father, he was rocking backwards and forwards like a mental case.

'. . . We therefore commit his body to be burned; earth to earth, ashes to ashes, dust to dust; looking for the general Resurrection in the last day, and the life of the world to come, through our Lord Jesus Christ . . .'

The coffin was gliding away while the organ music swelled up, the shining rollers taking it towards the far wall, where the small doors opened, and Connor went through. To be cremated, till nothing was left of him that anyone would ever recognise again.

Amber wanted to shout out; but she hadn't had the chance; it had all been the vicar's blah and a load of mushy religion. She wanted to do something other than stand here with Debra whimpering, her dad struggling as if he wanted the freedom to go through that door, too, and everyone in the chapel blowing their noses.

Connor! Love you, Connor! – that's what she wanted to shout; but now grief had robbed her of words, and she stood there shaking and silent.

Which was when Jonny Long suddenly tugged his escort sideways with a strong, violent heave and sent the man scrabbling. He leapt crouching onto the pew, twisting round to face everybody. 'Yeah!' Jonny shouted.

'Come down Long, be-have!' The escort was trying to get his balance back.

'You want to know who done that?' Jonny had a hand free for waving at where the coffin had been. 'You want to know who killed my boy? Do you?'

'Long!' The other prison officer grabbed at him.

'It was Mr P – he had him killed to take revenge on me! It was Mr P done it. An' if you want his full name, his real name, it's—' Which was when Jonny was pulled down; and only the people at the front heard the muffled 'Dimitris Papendreou' that he tried to shout out.

Some went this way, some went that. Jonny Long's escorting officers pulled him down the aisle and out through the front of the chapel. Shocked and staring, Amber and Debra were led out through the door at the front to walk past the floral tributes.

Sunil Dhillon and DC Webber watched Jonny Long being marched back to the car he'd come in – and Webber said to Dhillon quietly, 'You and me, off the record, let's talk.'

'Good idea,' said the trainee reporter. 'Where's your car?'

While rising above everyone, the smokeless emission from the crematorium furnace shimmered into the sky.

Chapter Nine

They sat in the front of the Vauxhall and watched the next funeral arrive. This was a bigger affair than young Connor Long's, with four following limousines and a line of private cars. The floral tributes spelt out 'MUM' along the side of the hearse and 'NAN' at the back, with the general grief spelt out by reddened faces and large handkerchiefs.

'Ever been to a Muslim funeral?' DC Webber asked Sunil Dhillon.

'Just Hindu!'

'It's only the men who go to the graveside. The women have to weep and wail back on the path!'

'It helps, a good wail. You Anglo-Saxons bottle it up – which does no good at all!'

Webber turned to Dhillon. 'So what did you make of Long's outburst in there?'

'Whatever, I guess it's why we were both there. We've both got questions about that death being an accident. You as police, me as press, even trainee! He looked directly at Webber. 'But as to who did it – I'm not in the loop enough to know what the father was on about over some Mr P...'

'I'll report it,' Webber deflected.

'Do you know who he was on about?'

The policeman shook his head.

'Did you see who was in the chapel, down the aisle on the left?'

'Who was that?'

'A black kid with trainer laces the same as those Connor Long was wearing when he died: blue in the left and red in the right...'

Webber frowned. 'Which means...?'

'Gang membership? Don't they do those sorts of things – twisted belts, off-centre buckles, bandanas, all those secret signs.'

'Not so secret then! I saw him – but I was more interested in who he was eyeballing...'

'What did I miss?'

Webber leaned a fraction closer to Sunil in a show of confidentiality. 'I think we could do each other a bit of good, you and me. That girl trusts you – you've met her; it was you told her about the witness Alfred Walters; she found the TV photograph of her brother for you.'

'It's only what we do...'

'That girl's convinced her brother was killed – and it could be her father was right as to who it was, this "Mr P" – but if you feed me what you get from her, like what the word is in the school and around the estate, I'll keep you up to speed where I can on what we're doing at division. She won't open up to police but she might to you; and at the end of the day you could have a nice little piece for your debut on *Panorama* . . .'

'What did I miss? Anyone significant?' Sunil Dhillon could be persistent.

'He was on the other side of the aisle to your laces boy. A youth called Alexandru Hajdu. Romanian. Suspected drugs pusher, small scale . . .'

'Romanian? I was at Stone Marsh Crown Court the other day, big drugs haul trial. The accused was a Romanian who was stopped by a road block at Bexley – after a tip-off to Revenue and Customs. Went down for ten years. Could it be Romanians in a drugs war with a Thames Reach lot?'

Webber jumped in quickly. 'Like the Barrier Crew? I'm not saying that. I'm not saying it's a drugs thing, I'm keeping an open mind.'

Sunil looked through the windscreen. 'I didn't tell you the entire truth. I wasn't here just as BBC. It's my morning off, and you haven't seen a camera or a notebook, have you?'

'She's a *schoolgirl*, man!'

'They're students at her age; and I was here partly because I wanted to be. But I guess a policeman's always a policeman – and a journalist's always a journalist . . .'

'Well, good for you. But if you come up with something from being friendly with young Amber, and if you'd like to run it by me, I can always confirm it or deny it for you . . .'

'Cheers.'

'Ian.'

'Cheers, Ian. Well, let's see how we go.'

'Sure. Let's do that.'

Sunil Dhillon got out of the car and went to find his scooter; while Ian Webber watched him ride off, then walked round to the back of the to note the names on the wreaths and the bouquets – before driving out of the grounds and down the A205 towards the Captain Cook, where Debra Long and her family and friends would be laying little Connor's ghost to rest with sandwiches and spirits.

Amber didn't want to be there. How could people do this sort of thing – coming straight from a kid's funeral into a pub? OK, the room they were in was private, but the music from the bar next door was loud, and once people had hugged each other there were more smiles on faces than tears. That would be all right for some old granddad who'd been seen off, or some tearaway dad who'd had a bit of a life: for them you could set up a row of drinks to drown your sorrows and say your thank-yous to everyone for turning up. But for Connor? All Amber wanted to do was go back to the flat and curl up on her bed in a tight little ball. But her mate Lauren had come with her – the only one there was room for in the funeral car – and although she'd shouted the name of the pub at the others, they probably wouldn't show up. This wasn't going to be anything pleasant, was it?

The Captain Cook was one of those places down by the Thames on the lower road that was still more pub than restaurant; and today it was hosting Debra's wake for Connor. Mourners came through the bar to the function room at the back, where glasses of sweet sherry and weak orange juice were already poured out; and on another table were measly sausage rolls, vol-au-vents with a prawn and a half in them, and greasy drumsticks with oily paper collars. The cheapest buffet on the list.

And there was Debra. However she'd managed to get through her son's funeral – greatly helped by Greek brandy – that was over now, and she was setting about drinking herself into forgetting. 'Stick the sherry!' she said to one of her cousins – and she sent him through to the bar to get her a gin and tonic. Soon the others were doing the same; and while the buffet table was cleared down to the torn paper tablecloth, the serious drinking began.

'What you going to do?' Amber asked Lauren. 'You want a drink, or shall we clear off?'

'Is there going to be a speech? You've got to stay for a speech.'

Amber looked around the room. The talk was all about her dad shouting out at the funeral, with a load of bravado from people who were definitely going to look into it; like, what was the villain's name? Mr P, or something? But before long their own lives were back in focus: the new patio being laid, the price of cheap flights, the nice-little-runner for sale: it soon stopped being about Connor, and there was no one who looked as if they wanted to make a speech.

'We'll go. We'll walk up the park, get a burger, and drop back to school . . .'

'School?' Lauren frowned. 'You seriously want to go back to T.R.A?'

'Anything normal.'

'What *was* that stuff your dad shouted out?'

Amber shrugged. There were things she would share with Lauren, and there were things she wouldn't. 'He was out of it, wasn't he?' But she had heard the Greek name.

'Hello!'

Amber caught the surprise in her mother's voice as someone came in through the door: a man of about twenty she'd seen around locally; mixed race in an expensive tracksuit.

'Sorry – thought I knew you.' Debra was swaying already. 'This is a private party. My little boy—'

'It's all right, Debs.' One cousin was speaking for several who would escort the intruder out. 'Can we help you, Sunshine?'

The newcomer ignored them all. 'Debra? Can I have

a word?' He dropped his voice as he gently twisted Amber's mother away from her protectors – who watched, and waited, and after a few moments when Debra turned back to call over her shoulder, 'Cyril – a large G an' T, there's a mate,' they started talking together again.

Amber sidled nearer as the man took her mother into a quieter corner.

'I got something to give you.' The man put his hand to an inside pocket of his jacket and took out an envelope, the business sort.

'You're not serving me notice on nothing, are you?'

'No, Debra – this is for you.' With which he closed her hand round the envelope and turned to walk out; while Debra stuffed whatever he'd given her into her funeral handbag.

'Who's he?' Amber wanted to know.

Debra was doing the shrugging now.

'What's he just given you?'

'Dunno.'

'Well, don't you *want* to know?'

"Course I do!' Debra suddenly snapped. 'In me own time – OK wi' you?'

'OK!' Something secret: from Winston, or some other man, perhaps helping out with cash for this nonsense.

'Leave off criticising. Right now we happen to be payin' our respects to Connor.'

Amber swore. 'Paying your respects? Right now you look like you're trying like hell to forget him!' And pushing her way through the noisy mourners, she led Lauren out into the street – in too much of a flounce to notice who was parked opposite the Captain Cook, on a meter in a Vauxhall: the detective constable who'd been very kind to her on the day Connor had died. But Webber's head was down for a second as he made a note of a character he'd just seen entering and leaving the pub, and the car he'd come in: a flash Toyota with a known face sitting waiting at its wheel.

Denny Benjamin.

'Well, I never,' he said to himself. 'Worth coming, then, Ian – worth coming.' And he looked up just after Amber and Lauren had disappeared round the corner.

School was different. School is always going to be different on the day a student has just said a last goodbye to a dead brother. Amber had felt grown up when she'd gone in to Thames Reach Academy after his murder; but today she had gone through what most of these teachers wouldn't know about till they were past retirement. She had scars: no, she had open wounds. Someone handing on experience? Take some of this! Lauren had been surprised she wanted to go that afternoon – and it was only partly for the reason Amber had given her, to do something normal. The other reason she couldn't share with even her best mate. She wouldn't admit it to anyone

– but she was going in because of Dawn Feldman.

Dawn Feldman had taken pity and been good to her over the holiday job – OK, and good to Lauren, too; but then she'd come to the flat the night Connor died, and spoken to Amber before even her mother had. And today she'd arranged for a beautiful bouquet from the school to be put on the top of Connor's hearse. Amber wanted to say thank you for that – and this afternoon was Mrs Feldman's session with her form.

In the form room the teacher looked at Amber and simply closed her eyes and opened them again; a private acknowledgment of Amber being there that day. But after deliberately not checking who was and who wasn't there – which was saying people could take or leave her sessions – Mrs Feldman took them along the corridor to the drama studio.

'Right, find a friend or sit this out,' she started.

Amber chose Lauren.

'I want you to think of some significant thing you or someone you know could've done, which can be true, or a stone-bonking lie, not some "nearly" thing. And nothing crackpot crazy, either, like playing up front for Arsenal . . .'

Which brought the usual cheers and jeers.

'You know what I'm on about. Think of a lie, or think of something true – and here you'll be top dog clever if you can think of something true that sounds like a lie . . .'

'I can't think of nothing,' Lee Manners whined. 'I've got a real boring life ...'

'Then let your mate go first.'

'He's got a boring life an' all.'

Which was not the case for Lauren. After a bit of thought she told Amber a story about her musician dad who sometimes played sax and clarinet at the Tramshed Sunday night jazz club in Woolwich. She and Amber went there sometimes, dancing on the crowded floor while her dad played a couple of sets. He knew lots of session musicians who work in recording studios, one of whom couldn't make it one day but needed the money, and her dad sat in for him on trumpet and ruined three 'takes' before being kicked out.

That was a lie, Amber decided. Even if the musician was a mate he wouldn't play a totally different instrument from his own; he'd probably give him the session money out of his own pocket, he wasn't short of a few bob. She had to say nothing yet, but for her turn she could only think of Connor, something wicked he'd done to the old boy next door – and in the end she sat down, she couldn't tell it.

Soon Dawn Feldman was clapping her hands. 'OK, what I want you to do before you tell your partner whether you told the truth or a lie, is think back to when you were telling your story. Think about body language. What was your partner doing when they were listening? Did they look away for a second or so?

Did their hand go to their ear, or did they scratch their chin? And when you were the listening one – did the teller's hands go to their face, which is a sign of lying, especially round the mouth; and when they'd finished, did they sort of brush themselves off? "Get away, lies!" Body language. These are the give-away things we do when we talk to one another. Can we trust people? Can people trust us? Are our lives truths or shams?'

Amber thought about what Lauren had done as she told her story. But that girl used her hands all the time when she was telling stuff, she could be folding origami the way her hands went at it – so there was no chance they ever went to her face. As for Amber scratching her own chin – *'chinny!'* – that's a known way of telling someone you don't believe them, and you usually do it on purpose.

'I reckon you believed me,' Lauren said. 'You didn't take your eyes off me, and you never scratched your chin.'

'Wrong. I didn't believe you. Your dad can't play trumpet so he couldn't pretend.'

'He can – he gave it up for clarinet – and that was a true story. It happened at a church they use for recording over the other side in Stratford. I could take you there . . .'

Amber looked round the drama studio. Some weren't doing this, they were talking about other stuff; but those who were, were either giving great explanations or accusing one another of telling lies.

'Who told you that trumpet story?' Amber asked.

'My dad did.'

'So you *think* it's true.'

'It *is* true!'

'What you think is true could be a lie, couldn't it? He could have put a bit on to a story that was nearly true. To you it's true because you believed him. But what's true to you could still be a lie, yes? How do you know he didn't make it up?'

'Because he's not that sort of man. I know my dad. He's not a dodgy character like yours!'

'Thanks very much.'

'No, Amb – I'm sorry. I owe you for that one. I see what you mean, but . . .'

'Forget it, Lor.'

'Anyhow, you wouldn't even tell me a story, lie *or* truth . . .'

'No.'

'Why not?'

Amber turned square to her. 'Because there's only one truth in the whole stinking world right now. I'd just say, "My brother got killed by someone who pushed him off a landing of Riverview House." And never mind what my hands or my nose or my chin or my ears were doing at the time, what would you say to that?' She stared into her friend's eyes.

Which didn't blink. 'I don't know, Amb. Is there body

language for saying "I don't know – but if you believe it, I want to believe it with you"?'

Amber went on staring. 'Yes,' she said, eventually. 'You just being my mate.'

Dawn Feldman came over; she'd been going round the groups. 'It's about trust,' she said. 'Truth and trust.' Amber could tell she was deliberately keeping this straight, normal – which was what she had wanted in coming to school. 'In films you can trust a performance where the actor – the *actor* – is telling the truth. Most actors are lying anyway: because they're pretending, already they're sort of lying. But then some give performances that you know contain the truth, and you can trust them . . .'

Amber stood up as if she hadn't taken in a word of what Mrs Feldman had just said. 'I want to thank you for the flowers,' she said. 'They helped me a lot today—'

'I'm pleased. We wanted to do it.' The teacher looked round to check there was time to say something else, quietly. 'This place is a *big* old family – but it *is* a family. And we're all your family, Amber . . .'

'Thanks.' Amber stared into the teacher's eyes, and the teacher stared back. And the biggest surprise of that afternoon in Thames Reach Academy was when Amber started to cry, and with an arm around her, Dawn Feldman cried, too, and the pair of them silenced the noisy studio.

Chapter Ten

The senior reporter was saying his piece to camera. 'The electrical failure lasted until well after the morning rush hour should have been over. Replacement buses failed to cope in the congestion that followed, and transport chiefs – and the mayor's office – are left to think very hard about how a faulty switch could bring central London to a standstill. This is Dermot Mark for BBC London News in the City.'

Mark admired his reflection in the big brown lens until Steve the cameraman called, 'Cut', holding on to the arm of the London Underground executive he'd just interviewed while the trainee got word from the studio that the package had gone down the line successfully. Sunil nodded.

Dermot Mark signed an autograph and thanked the London Underground executive. The man walked away as Sunil's mobile rang.

'It's Amber. Amber Long. Can I see you?'

'Of course. I said any time. When?'

'Soon as? You were at Connor's thing this morning. You heard my dad, what he shouted out . . .?'

'Everyone did.'

'It's about that.'

'OK. I've got to be at the BBC till eleven tonight; not the normal London News place – we're at TV Centre for a couple of weeks. But I could slip out to see you in reception . . .'

'How do I get there?'

'Come to White City Underground – the trains are running again now – cross the road to the TV Centre, and ask for me. I'll leave word at the desk.'

'OK.'

And Sunil clicked off his phone. Amber had been lucky to get through – he normally kept it off while Dermot Mark was interviewing; and he'd been lucky she hadn't rung four minutes earlier and ruined a take.

Sitting at his computer in the CID office Ian Webber was reading the pages he'd called up on the court case Sunil Dhillon had talked about – while across in their section of the office a couple of sergeants were back-slapping a promotion – Liz Kwayana had passed her board and been made up to Detective Inspector, transferring to one of the squads at New Scotland Yard.

'Can't call you "Liz" any more – it'll have to be "Guv" from now on.'

'It'd better be "Ma'am", boy, or I'll have you up for sexual har-ass-ment!'

'With the accent on the "ass".'

They all laughed – but judging by the way she looked at them, already she was someone else. Seeing Webber trying to ignore the celebration she left her group to go over to him.

'What you got there, Ian?'

'What the BBC is onto already, it seems. Drugs. That Dartford case. A Romanian link. Have you heard of a Romanian outfit operating out of the West End?'

'Come on, Ian – the big players are for the Yard, what do you want with that, out here on division? You seen the local unsolved crime list?'

'A known Romanian boy showed himself yesterday, lives along Thames Street. He was at Connor Long's funeral – eyeballing another local lad across the chapel. And the last person to see Connor alive now remembers he saw him running as if he was being chased.' Webber pointed a finger at the computer screen. 'It'd be a feather in our cap if we nailed someone distributing down here . . .' Webber looked up at her meaningfully.

Liz Kwayana leaned over and rudely closed down the page. 'Leave it. You got enough on – don't go looking for glory where you don't have to.'

Webber pushed his keyboard away from him. He stood up, looked across at the sergeants laughing amongst themselves, excluding him from the celebration: so he signed-out downstairs. He drove his car into Greenwich, parked, and walked through the foot tunnel under the Thames, to sit quietly and stare at one of the world's best views – of Wren's naval college and the Royal Observatory.

Something uplifting. Looking for glory was a rotten way of describing how he saw his job.

Alexandru Hajdu lived above the Chicky-Chick takeaway on Thames Street, in a Victorian terrace where rats bred. In a side turning opposite, Ian Webber was in his car, parked on a yellow line. This side of Thames Street had already been developed and the residents of the modern apartments on either side of him had their own parking in the courtyards within; a traffic warden was unlikely to patrol along here. The DC had changed into the surveillance clothes he kept in his boot: his fawn baseball cap without logo, his leather bomber jacket, scruffy jeans, and cheap trainers from JJB. Now he sat and watched the building opposite. It was early evening and Chicky-Chick was fairly busy. The schoolkids had gone home, and the after-pub trade was still indoors getting ready to go out, but the takeaway's door was constantly opening and closing.

From the knowledge Webber had, most evenings Alex Hajdu could be seen around the teen hang-outs in Lewisham, Greenwich, or Thames Reach. But it was an hour before he came out of the private door at the side of the takeaway. He was in a long black leather coat over a white open-necked shirt and ironed jeans, grey trainers, and he had a Nike gymsack slung across his body, filled with something or other.

Webber pulled down his cap and eased himself out of his car, taking a long time pretending to lock it while he watched Alex Hajdu walk off east – and suddenly run for a 472 bus going to Thamesmead. Immediately, Webber was into his car and negotiating his exit from the side turning to get after the bus, catching up with it a car or two back, just beyond the next stop.

It's never easy, following a bus. Webber couldn't use the 'follow by leading' trick where he'd get in front, because Hajdu could get off the bus at any time and Webber wouldn't see him do it. So he had to stay behind – which annoys other road users, the car constantly pulling over while a bus keeps stopping. But that's what he had to do; and he kept in touch – ignoring the odd hoot from an exasperated driver.

He kept his eyes keen on the 472, and Hajdu didn't get off, and didn't get off. It looked as if he was heading for Thamesmead. He followed the bus all the way. It had come along Thames Street packed with commuters from North Greenwich underground station, people getting off in New Charlton, Woolwich, and Crossway, but Webber was absolutely certain Hajdu hadn't been among them. So it had to be Thamesmead town centre he was heading for – and that seemed to fit the bill perfectly. If Hajdu was into drugs, Thamesmead would be a likely place to operate, because despite the best efforts of its decent residents, there was a big drugs problem among its youth. Not for the first time would Webber's cap be shielding eyes trained on a Thamesmead block of flats.

As the 472 pulled up at the final bus stop, Webber stopped about fifteen metres short of it, ready to leave the car and follow on foot. But no Alexandru Hajdu got off. Webber shot out of his car and ran to a shop doorway to look the bus over – and the only person on the vehicle was the driver, sitting filling in a time sheet.

'Blast!' Because that meant Hajdu had pulled a stroke. He had got on the 472 and got off it again way back at the very next stop along Thames Street – the only time he could have done it: Webber had seen every other stop, the full length of the route. But Hajdu couldn't have known he was going to be followed. What he'd done that evening was part of his routine. And how many upright, law-abiding citizens with nothing to hide ever do that sort of thing, Liz Kwayana?

Amber always got a buzz from seeing someone famous walking the streets or filming around the O_2; and sitting on one of the sofas in the TV Centre reception, Amber saw Willy Falco going through with a gawky woman talking seriously at him. It was quite a jolt to see a man who won all the comedy awards looking as if he was being given grief. But that early sight was all there was to see of interest; she had to wait a long time, and no one else she recognised came out of the lifts. Except, finally, Sunil Dhillon. Suddenly, there he was.

'Amber . . .'

'Hi!'

'Sorry, I couldn't get away.'

But he looked quite pleased with himself about that. And Amber took in the matte make-up on his forehead. If she'd bothered to look at the monitors she might have seen him just now on television: Sunil Dhillon the pro.

'Anti-shine. Sorry. Couldn't get out because they let me do a postscript on the half-past ten.' He wiped at the make-up with a tissue. 'Good to see you. But a very difficult day for you. I thought this morning was—'

'Interesting. Are you going to say "interesting"?'

Sunil sat. 'No, I'm not. It was moving, and it was real, and sad – tragic – and you held your head up and I think you did your brother proud . . .'

'And this is you talking?'

'Who else?' He looked uncomfortable. 'And I can excuse your dad . . .'

'*Excuse?* My dad's torn in half. He's carrying a ton of guilt – knowing Connor was killed because he didn't do what he was told . . .'

'OK.' Sunil slid them both along the sofa, further away from others. 'What was that all about?'

Amber told him. 'My dad went inside for working-over an airport man who didn't pay what he owed to that Mr P he shouted about – a punishment he had to dish out to pay off his gambling debts. But once he was in prison he got another order from the man – taken in by my mum, would you believe? – telling him he hadn't done enough to pay up everything he owed; not every last pound. He'd got to do a punishment on someone else, some other prisoner.'

Sunil Dhillon didn't interrupt.

'But my dad didn't do it, didn't carry it out. Don't ask me why, I don't know him that well. Then Mr P—'

Ambers words caught in her throat, because flashing into her head was the sight of little Connor's chalk outline on that concrete – as fresh an image as when she'd first knelt over it – 'Mr P punished my dad by hitting at his family . . .'

'Do you know his full name?'

'Only from the funeral. Where I was, I heard what my dad said. Dimitris Papen-something . . .'

'So the theory is, this Papen-something had your brother pushed off that balcony . . .?'

'*Theory?*' Amber rounded on him. 'It's what he *did*! You heard him. My dad's solid certain that's what happened to Connor.'

Sunil made calming movements with his hands. 'OK. I'm with you; trust me, I don't think this is crazy talk . . .' He looked down at the carpet; people were staring at them. 'We all picked that up in the chapel.'

'So, what does Amber Long want, you're asking . . .'
Sunil looked her in the face: said nothing.

'I'm asking you to find out where this man lives.
Big name in gambling. Must be easy to find . . .'

'No problem. I can do that. Then what? Are you going
to go and sort him out . . .?'

'You *wouldn't*, for your little brother?'

For a second Sunil looked as if he was about to pat
Amber on the knee. 'You need to have a bit more savvy
than risk spending ten or fifteen years of your own life
in prison.'

'Anything's worth it.' *What did this Sunil Dhillon
know?*

'You need to be sure, for a start. And then you need
to work the system . . .'

'Oh, the system!' Amber wanted to stand up and
shout at him. 'What system could the likes of me work?
What chance do council estate people get to play any
toff system in this country?'

'. . . I'm here at the BBC,' Sunil said, 'there's television
exposure – that can be very effective. And Ian Webber's
there: Amber, he didn't go to Connor's funeral to watch
for pickpockets. We're both parts of the way things
work. What you can't do is just go taking revenge on
someone who could be the wrong person anyway.'

Amber swung round on him. 'The wrong person?
After what I've told you? That information came from
my mum and my dad – and rotten toe-rags they might

be, but they don't make up stuff like that . . .'

Sunil stood. 'How are you getting home?'

'The same way I came.' Amber knew he was only trying to be sensible, he was saying the sort of stuff an older brother would say. Putting the other side of the argument, like in the book Dawn Feldman had read from.

'Will your mother worry till you get in?'

'No chance. She won't be in for three days.'

'I go past your place. Fancy a lift on the back of my scooter?'

'You got two crash helmets?'

'Good point. Yeah, I've got an old one in my locker.'

'All right, then.' She did need Sunil Dhillon's help. She had come here to ask him to get the address of Dimitris Papend-something, and she was determined to get it.

'And we'll have a kebab and a coke by the Cutty Sark . . .'

'Oh, yes?' Amber smiled at him. 'Who's paying?'

'I could swing it on the BBC . . .'

Instantly, the smile left her face 'Which would mean you're doing this professionally . . .?'

He was caught in a half move towards the lifts. 'I'm just me,' he said, 'and my work and all the other stuff I do are just parts of me.' He came back to her. 'I stood looking at an autocue tonight reading words I didn't write, but I made them sound as if I had. I lie to my mum about her chicken madras but that doesn't mean

I don't love her to bits. I don't draw lines dividing the different parts of my life. I'm me – and you're you. I know you because we met while I was doing my job. OK – because of that do you want me to work out the percentage of petrol I use taking you a mile out of my way to Thames Reach, and separate my journey from yours?' He smiled at her. 'If you've got qualms about the meal, I'm paying, OK?' The smile left his face. 'But do I put the minutes I might spend thinking about you on my timesheet, or in my personal diary, or both? Or neither?' He stood to mock attention in front of her. 'Are you Amber Long?'

'Yes.'

'I'm Sunil Dhillon. All of me. Going home?'

'Yes.'

'Great. Three minutes to get your helmet.' And he hurried over to catch a departing lift.

Chapter Eleven

Amber wouldn't recommend a ride through central London on the back of a scooter to anyone with a weak heart. The natural urge was to cling onto Sunil in front but he told her not to – no offence, but it was safer to hold the rack behind her. The one-way system from Wood Lane through to Fulham wasn't so bad, but when they hit the Embankment and the Old Kent Road, buses and delivery lorries loomed large on both sides, and when Amber's nose started to run in the chilly slipstream, there was no way she could spare a hand to cuff it. It was some relief when Sunil pulled over and parked on the pavement in Greenwich town centre, chaining the scooter to a road sign.

'OK?' he took off his helmet and smiled at Amber.

'Fine.'

'Enjoy it?'

'Great.'

'If it's a regular thing, two up, you can get helmets with intercoms. Have a chat as you go along.'

'Nice.' A regular thing? *That* would never be a regular thing! You learn fast, though. Amber had soon picked

129

up that when he leaned forward over his handlebars he was going to put on a spurt, make it through some gap – so she gripped the rack at her back all the harder, leaning into him. And she soon got the hang of going with him when he leaned to one side or the other. But what she learnt overall was something else. Trust. He was the rider, she was the passenger. Her life was in his hands, and she had to trust him with it.

He had stopped outside an Indian restaurant, not a kebab house. 'Do you mind? It's nicer for sitting, inside.'

He was right. Kebab houses had tables where you could grab a meal. Indian restaurants had alcoves where you could eat one in comfort. And the Taj Mahal would be more private than Kebab Ye for the sort of talk Amber wanted. She followed Sunil in, dangling her helmet like a regular pillion rider.

The place wasn't busy, but Sunil was shown to a laid-up recess too close to the kitchen archway for his liking, so he picked another nearer to the street, where he could keep an eye on his scooter. He was a bit like Lauren's dad in restaurants, Amber thought; not being satisfied with where he was put.

They sat opposite one another. The menus came fast, and the ordering was quick, chicken madras for them both, with chapattis and dips and two Coca-Colas to be going on with. The meat of the conversation had to wait, though: all the time the waiter came and went there was no way Amber could launch into Mr P.

'How do you get to be a reporter?' she asked Sunil.

'"You" meaning anyone, or "you" meaning me?'

'There's a difference?' Amber fiddled with her linen napkin.

'There's a definite difference.' Sunil widened his eyes at her. 'My mum, she's the difference. For her I had to be a lawyer so I went to Sussex to do Law, and switched to Media and Cultural studies when she wasn't looking.'

'My mum wouldn't care whether I did Law or lap-dancing . . .'

'I don't think Sussex offers that. Except in Brighton in the evenings . . .'

'It's near Brighton, your uni?'

'Bus ride, or bike. "London by the sea", they call it, you've got whatever you want there. Plus the South Downs at the back, the open air, the beaches, freedom all around . . .' Sunil waved an arm at all the freedom.

Amber frowned.

'. . . The freedom of being a student. Yes, your work, your lectures, your dissertations – but your friends, no responsibility for a few years, plenty of mucking-about time, that's what it's all about. Finding yourself.'

'I've got no trouble finding me. I'm always in the shit.' But Amber said it lightly, her face a muscle more open now. 'Then you went to the BBC?'

Cutlery was being laid, dish warmers brought, water poured. Mr P was still a serving away.

'I got on a local paper in Leicester where my uncle

lives, then I got to be a trainee at BBC Radio Midlands, and came back to London as a trainee in the local pool.'

'But not in at the deep end?'

Sunil laughed, a genuine yelp. 'Amber Long,' he said, gurgling on Coke as if he was too shy to say it straight, 'I like your style.'

'Thank you very much.' Which she meant as a put-down. She should have got what she wanted from this guy while they were at the BBC. Amber knew he liked her style – or her looks – that had been in his eyes from the time he'd brought back Connor's photograph: like most of her mates, she could read that sort of thing.

'What about you? What are you going to do after next year?'

Amber shrugged. He knew her age, he knew her year in school, he knew where she was in life – numerically. He'd probably worked out that he could kiss her without going to prison for it.

'What do your teachers say you should do?'

She shrugged again. Even Dawn Feldman hadn't got to that yet.

'Well, let me tell you this –' And Sunil leaned so far over the table towards her that the waiter coming with the food pretended he'd forgotten something and went back to the counter '– You've got a spirit, and you've got a quest. You're in the depths of a tragedy, and you've got the killing of a family member to sort . . .'

He'd said it; he'd actually laid it out in words! Connor

hadn't had an accident – he'd been deliberately killed.

'. . . But don't let that end *your* life, too. You've got a brain, Amber, and you can go anywhere you want—'

'Two chicken madras . . .?' The food couldn't wait for ever. Their curries were put in front of them, the vegetables on the warmer were waved at. 'Enjoy your meal.'

Now, with some sort of privacy likely to last for a few minutes, Amber came to the crux of seeing Sunil Dhillon. Information about Mr P – that was what she was here for. Round a hot mouthful, she asked him. 'You meant it when you said you'd find out about Mr P . . .?'

'I meant it, and I did it.' His hand went to an inside pocket. 'I got the name and address when I went up for your helmet . . .'

It was not her helmet. It was his spare.

'Here . . .' He held out a small memo sheet, torn from a pad. 'Dimitris Papendreou. He lives in Cockfosters Road. The end of the Piccadilly line. Turning right out of Cockfosters station you've got the entrance to Trent Park, and then crossing the road there are these big, gated houses further along on the left-hand side. A place called Acropolis.' He was staring at her, hard. 'That's for your father to know, or his lawyers. But you leave it at that. "Revenge is a kind of wild justice; which the more man's nature runs to the more ought law to weed it out."'

133

'I thought you didn't do Law.'

Sunil laid down his cutlery. 'That's a quote – but this information I'm giving you is to show you where I'm coming from. To let you know I'm on your side.'

'Thanks.' *Let go!* He was still holding on to a corner of the memo sheet.

'Just don't do anything silly. So far you've only got your dad's word for how deep-in this man is. There are other possibilities for what happened to Connor . . .'

Amber's stomach rolled. It wasn't just her: it was reckoned by this reporter from the BBC. Twice. Connor had been murdered.

Sunil finally let go of the paper. 'Like the man said – enjoy your meal.'

But, to be honest – and in spite of Sunil's shining eyes and smiling mouth – the word *enjoy* was nowhere in Amber's vocabulary: and it wouldn't be for a long time to come. She said nothing, though. When you live on the Barrier Estate you know how to keep your mouth shut: and especially when you're sitting across the table from a television reporter, even a trainee.

Ian Webber sat in his car opposite Chicky-Chick again; but as long as he waited, and late as it was, Alex Hajdu didn't come back to his flat. If he was dropping off drugs like a milkman on a night round he might well be out till the early hours. Webber had to get his sleep but he didn't want to end the night with nothing to show for his efforts. He locked his car and crossed Thames Street to the takeaway.

'Hi, boss.'

'Hi.' Webber was the only customer. He looked up at the picture gallery of options sited above the grills and hotplates: looked up, and around, taking in the two Asian men in red-and-white chequered paper hats behind the counter. 'Got a chicken breast anywhere, mate? All these legs must've held something off the ground . . .' He'd have a meal waiting at home, but he didn't want to be a copper in here.

'Sure.' The older man went to a rotisserie in the corner where a couple of scrawny chicken breasts were turning and dripping. 'Chips?'

'Small.'

A box was quickly made up and his meal placed on the counter.

'Is Alex Hajdu usually this late?' Webber waved a casual hand at the ceiling.

The younger man's eyes focused. 'This is takeaway,' he said. '*Food* takeaway. We don' deal in nothing else.'

'I know. Sorry.' Webber took the rebuke the way he was meant to, with a look of shame. 'It's just I owe him, an' I wondered if anyone was indoors upstairs . . .'

'Separate premises.' The older man wanted him out. He rang up the cost of a chicken breast and chips and held out his hand for the money.

Webber paid him with a twenty and a tenner. 'Keep the change,' he said.

The man eyed him, hesitated; but his son put the money in the till. 'Pete's in, boss.'

'Peter Hajdu?'

The son nodded.

'How old?'

Now a shrug. 'Sixteen, eighteen . . . Goes to school.'

'Thames Reach?'

'Wears them clothes.'

'Thanks.' Webber left it at that; picked up his supper and went for the door. 'I'll come back some other time.'

'But no parking ticket for six months, eh, boss?' the son smiled.

Webber walked out. So much for not being the copper, then.

The flat was dark and empty when Amber got in. She hadn't let Sunil see her up to her landing; told him that Bartram House girls weren't scared of their own lifts and staircases, thanks. She couldn't work Sunil out. She knew he fancied her – any fool could see he'd got eyes for her like a watching dog. So was that where he was coming from? Or was his job the truth part of it? He was a reporter, he *had* to have a pro interest in the Longs, it'd be stupid to think any other way. In which case would that be for a sensational news item interest, or for a serious programme he wanted to set up for

Dermot Mark: the sort where reporters dig up stuff to put money crooks and snake-gang bosses behind bars? Amber didn't know – so she stopped thinking about it. What she wanted now was to set her alarm, get into bed, and wake up in time to choose what to do with her Friday, clear-headed. Would she go to school, or go to see where Papendreou lived so that she could start planning how to get back at him? What had Sunil called it – *wild justice*? Well, she was wild enough to do something all right. This was all about revenging Connor; her Connor, whose body had gone up in smoke today.

She went into his small bedroom. The room had never been this neat when he was alive. Not that he'd ever had much stuff of his own to make it untidy. He'd got an old Playstation that didn't work, a rubber Spiderman, and some kids' DVDs that she'd never known him to watch. But there were no posters on the door or the wall – he'd never been into bands, or football. He'd liked comics, the older sort, and she'd sometimes hear him snort with a laugh – but when she went in to find out what had creased him up, it was never anything that tickled her; it would usually be too horrible for that. Now, cleaned and tidied, the place just seemed as if Connor had gone away for a while. His empty room.

Amber wanted to cry. She turned to get out. If she cried in here she'd break down completely – and she wasn't going to do that: tonight she was going to keep control. She switched off the light. But, hold on, what was that, tidied under a snowstorm paperweight on his chest of drawers? What tatty scrap of paper was that? Had she seen that before? If she had, she hadn't noticed it. She put the light on again.

It was a mobile phone top-up voucher worth five pounds on the T-mobile system. Which meant that it wasn't Debra's, she was on O_2, and it wasn't her own, she was with Orange; and it wasn't her father's because he hadn't earned the right to use his mobile in Marwood. So had Connor got himself another mobile phone? He'd lost his Christmas present – and as far as she knew he'd never had the money to get another: she'd certainly never seen one. Also, if he'd had another mobile he'd have put that same, loud, stupid ring tone on it, and roll around the floor laughing at the Crazy Frog, however many times he heard it. No, if this voucher had been Connor's he'd kept his new mobile ultra, ultra secret.

Which was something else to keep Amber awake, going to bed with the door unbolted just in case Debra decided to come home.

Chapter Twelve

Detective Constable Webber had plenty to do that Friday. The Blackheath flasher, who was a resident in a mental health after-care hostel, had to be interviewed; a market trader in Woolwich had to be arrested on suspicion of selling stolen watches, and a DVD pirate in Powis Street still had to be charged – with every Hollywood film on his plastic sheet needing to be verified as an illegal copy. So with all the coming and going and typing up entailed in those three cases, Webber didn't have much time for off-task phone calls. But he made one. It was to the HM Revenue and Customs officer at Scotland Yard who'd organised the Bexley roadblock that had snared the Romanian Andre Basescu carrying those kilos of cocaine in the boot of his BMW. Now, with Liz Kwayana out of the office, Ian Webber got through to him and was allowed to come to the point of his call.

'I know you're working on the evidence, and I know you want to nail the Mr Big . . .' he started to say.

But, 'What crap TV stuff have you been watching, son? "Mr Big!" You're talking about some swarthy arsehole with a lock-up and a mobile phone.'

'It's his skin I'm after, sir, not its colour,' Webber shot back – which was not a good start. 'But I've got a small-fry Romanian pusher on my patch, and I could actually be some help in what you're doing.'

'What's his name?'

'Alexandru Hajdu.'

'You know how many Romanians we've got over here? And who says any bent ones all have to work for one boss?'

'Not someone called Răz? No one ever found who Basescu was shouting about in court?'

'We don't think that was a name. He was telling us where to go – something like that . . .'

Webber kept his face straight – and therefore his voice. 'It's just the chance of something clicking – like catching a killer because he's pulled for a minor offence . . .'

'Don't tell *me* police work, son. What do you want to know?' The man's voice went away as if he was checking the position of the 'call ended' button.

'Just where the tip-off came from. If you know it. If it's one of yours, undercover, obviously you can't tell me, but if it's–'

Webber was stopped by a snort. '"*Undercover?*" Do more reading, constable, watch less television!'

'That's good advice, sir, but–'

'It was a phone call. Out of the blue. Could have been

140

something, could have been nothing – we never know till after, do we?'

'You're right, we don't.'

'But this one confirmed some stuff we knew. The call came from . . .' Webber heard the clack of a keyboard. 'Listen, this is a pain, you know that? It's come to trial, the man's gone down, we're going back a bit here . . .'

'I'm very grateful, sir.'

'Hang on. Here it is.' There was a pause, then: 'The call came from a Telecom public phone in Deptford High Street.'

'Deptford High Street?'

'There can't be many left any more, so you can put on your camouflage and stake it out.'

Webber ignored the sarcasm. 'What about the voice giving the tip-off? Does the record show any clue on the accent?'

'Wait. Yes, we've got something there. *Sarf* London, it's reckoned. Strong – not the accent, the tone. And he used a Jamaican word for cocaine so he could be black, which means you can take your pick, round your way.'

Webber was making his left-handed notes. 'Then one theory that could hold up is . . . we've got drugs outfit "A" fingering drugs outfit "B" in some sort of turf war . . .'

'You're at it again, James Bond. But I'll give you this – suppose outfit "A" is suffering from outfit "B" muscling in on their supply route – too many snouts in the trough . . .?'

'Which would be our locals suffering because of the Romanians getting in at Dartford . . .'

'But then outfit "A" opens up a different supply route – wherever that might be . . .'

'Yes . . .'

'Then it fits up the other one as it pulls out: like fouling the doorstep when you move house.'

'I try never to do that, sir,' Webber said – an attempt at a joke; but Revenue and Customs coughed, a smoker sounding ready for a puff outside. 'But don't go looking for facts to fit a theory; just have it in the back of your mind. Go from what you've got, not what you wish you'd got – otherwise what you're doing is working arse-about-face. They ought to teach you that at Hendon.'

'It's more in line with what they taught me at Cambridge, sir. Lateral thinking. But I hear what you're saying. Thank you very much for your time.'

The line was already dead. Which left Webber to hang up the phone, go back to his computer, and call up what he'd got on known south London Afro-Caribbean fly-boys. Where suddenly halfway down one of his lists a name seemed to highlight itself; a name with a mug-shot attachment to it: a face Webber had seen only the day before, waiting in his car outside the Captain Cook: Billy Dawson's muscle.

'Well, I never,' he said softly to his screen. 'Denny Benjamin . . .'

Amber's phone rang before her alarm went off. It woke her from a deep sleep of no dreams. It was Lauren.

'Amb – have you seen the *Sun*?'

'Haven't opened the curtains yet. What the hell time is it?'

'The *paper*, Sleeping Beauty. Front page. Big stuff. It's about your dad and what he shouted at the funeral . . .'

'Oh, my God! Read it out! Read it out!' Amber was up, feet on the floor, light on.

'Can't. Oki rang and told me. But get one, Amb – she said it's front page. *Front page, girl!*'

'I will. I'm going. I'll see you later . . .'

'Yeah, see you later. Oki says it reads like he's in a right strop.'

'My dad?'

'Some long Greek name. Picture, everything . . .'

'I'm out of here. I'm getting one. Thanks, Lor . . .' And, within minutes, pulling on a tracksuit, no wash, Amber was in the lift and hitting Roland Street for Mr Shah's News and General Store.

They knew who she was in there; but there wasn't a word said to her when she bought the paper. Again, the same as after Connor's death, at times like this no one seemed to know what to say. The popular papers were laid along the counter, and a quick look told Amber it was only the *Sun* that had the funeral story.

DEAD KID'S DAD SMEARS CASINO BOSS

The headline was big and heavy, with a picture of a stern Dimitris Papendreou staring through thick black glasses.

Mrs Shah took Amber's money, and Amber folded the paper inwards to hurry back to the flat to read the *Sun* 'exclusive' – knowing what exclusive meant: that someone had sold the paper this story.

Violent Jonny Long, serving five years for GBH, disrespected his **DEAD BOY'S** funeral to shout **MURDER** yesterday. Cuffed to a prison officer he leapt on a **PEW** at the south London **CREMATORIUM** to accuse gambling chief **DIMITRIS PAPENDREOU** of masterminding son **CONNOR'S** fatal fall from **RIVERSIDE HOUSE**, Thames Reach.

Go to page 7

Amber tore through the pages to a column inside.

From page 1
Dimitris Papendreou, whose **GAMBLING CHAIN** includes London, Brighton and Croydon **CASINOS**, plus a string of **BETTING SHOPS**, denied Long's dramatic claim – which the cuffed prisoner shouted out before being **STIFLED** by prison officers and **FROGMARCHED** out of the chapel.

"I'm no killer,' Mr Papendreou told the *Sun*. 'I'm a businessman and a family man, and this crazy claim is in the hands of my solicitors.'

Connor Long, **TEN**, who fell from a block of flats ten days ago was cremated minutes after the outburst.

And there, in the middle of the column, was a small picture of Connor – smiling into his own mobile phone last Christmas. Amber spread the paper flat on the

144

kitchen table, pulled up a chair with her foot, and sat with her head in her hands. She swore, violently; because this was not the picture Debra had given to the local papers: it was the picture Amber had found especially for the BBC: the one she had given to Sunil Dhillon.

Sunil Dhillon. She'd told him the important first bit of the name her dad had tried to shout out – the sweet-talking twicer! The traitor! The reporter who was showing he worked in the gutter, no better than the lowest of the low-life who live off other people's tragedies. They couldn't put this story on the BBC without any film so he'd done a deal and sold it privately to the *Sun. Trust!* The bastard had sat talking to her in the Taj Mahal as if he was her best friend; he'd stared her in the face and told her she had style, told her not to go looking for revenge – when all the time he knew he was selling this stuff to a national newspaper. How could she have trusted a man like this – who'd fooled his own mother and switched courses from Law to peddling stories round the media? So who were the real crooks around here? Well, she'd sort Sunil Dhillon later. But for today Thames Reach Academy didn't stand a chance of seeing Amber Long – not against the possibility of her finding this Papendreou apology for a human being. She'd got the details Dhillon had given her – so that was where she'd go today. She'd bang at his front door and shove his weasel newspaper words down his throat, give him something to think about. Because she was going to use any bit of brain God had given her to get back at him for what he'd done to Connor. Then let his family put that in the hands of his solicitors . . .

Cockfosters in the north of London was a very different world from the one Amber knew. She'd been born a few streets from where she lived; all her life she'd walked pavements of gum and spit, breathing air that smelled of the world's leftovers. Even along by the Thames with its broad open space, on a bad day when the wind blew off a low tide it could stink like a sewer; and up on wide Blackheath the roads were always thick with exhaust. But here on a warm spring morning the traffic was sparse, the sun was clear, and the air smelt of the country.

Amber walked from the Underground station looking for the house called Acropolis. Sitting in the tube she'd stared over and over at that *Sun* headline in people's hands. Who *could* she trust any more? Lauren, yes, best friend. Debra, no – she was anyone's for a gin and tonic. Her own dad – don't ask – the weak idiot. Dawn Feldman – definitely. While Sunil Dhillon she wouldn't trust with a used Oyster card.

In the open now as she walked past the gates of Trent Park and along Cockfosters Road, Amber's mind fixed itself on that hard face in the paper. They'd deliberately found a picture of Papendreou looking glinty-eyed and like someone you wouldn't want to upset; smiling ever so slightly, yes – but like the sort of world leader you saw on television who had more weapons of mass destruction than anyone else; the face of a tyrant who would bounce his baby on his knee while his men did terrible things down in the torture chamber. Arms' length – that's where he kept the dirty work; so getting at a man like that wouldn't be easy. The twittering of the birds and the sound of a motor mower all seemed so *right*: while what was ordered to go on from behind the walls of one of these posh houses was so wrong. Amber had no doubt that Mr P's hands were kept clean; but his soul had to be as dirty as they get.

She crossed the road after the right-hand path ran out – which was a pity because she'd have had a better view of Acropolis from the other side. Keeping tight to the walls she passed large house after large house, each one different from the previous; red brick, yellowed stone, white plastered; until, suddenly, here it was. She was at a gate with stone lions sitting on top of the pillars. And there in Greek-style lettering but in the English alphabet was the name, set in a different coloured marble. ACROPOLIS.

She caught her breath and her heart missed a beat; a burst of adrenalin screwed her stomach. Cautiously, she peered through the ironwork to get a first look at the house – which was as big as a hotel, with town hall columns, and tinted windows reflecting back the sun. There were no cars on the curved driveway – Papendreou was probably at work watching someone's balls being roasted by a blow torch – so she couldn't knock on the door and shout at him, which was a pisser. And suddenly there was an Alsatian running from the side of the house, snarling and barking at her through the gate. When she didn't move it threw its weight at the ironwork, black gums wet, eyes alight, its beast of a body pushing to get at her.

'Get lost!' But Amber's legs shook at the shock as she retreated behind the wall. Upset and angry, she shouted abuse at the beast; but when the barking had stopped she breathed deeply to recover her calm. Anyone with eyes could see through Dimitris Papendreou, showing himself up for what he was; he had to be a man with loads of enemies to need a killer dog patrolling his grounds. And now Amber had one thing sorted in her mind; even from this first look and the feel of the house, she knew her revenge would have to be taken somewhere else; at one of Papendreou's casinos, or betting shops, or in traffic.

But she hadn't come this far just to walk away so soon. Ready for the dog this time, Amber was going to give it something to bark at. Safe on her side of the grill she suddenly jumped back into view and rattled the gate like some demented prisoner, shouting every doggish swear word she could invent. Here came the Alsatian again, racing at her, barking louder, lashing itself at the gate as she waved at it, and pulled faces, and shouted and screeched. Like before, she stepped back, while the dog barked on longer this time; then, when it was quiet, and with the devil on her face, she jumped in front of the gate to do it all again: until, with the dog going crazy at Amber's taunting body and foul language, a man's head came angrily over the wall of the place next door.

'Oi! Sling your effing hook, will you?'

Amber turned from the maddened dog. 'Sling your own!' she shouted back: but left it at that. Pulling herself straight, she walked away from the Greek's gate and back past this other man's house to head for the station; telling herself that people out here weren't as different from Thames Reach people as they pretended.

Chapter Thirteen

Billy Dawson's Midnight Express nightclub kept a rackety white Ford van for its bits and pieces of running about. It was mostly one of the bouncers or a barman who drove it, but sometimes Denny Benjamin would take the wheel, on a very low profile drive. And certainly that Friday afternoon, no one would be taking much notice of Benjamin driving it along the A233 from Bromley towards Westerham on a minor route that crossed the M25 – except DC Ian Webber in his Vauxhall, which was tailing him at a safe distance.

The Ford kept strictly within the speed limit and from two or three cars back Webber had no trouble staying in touch. Denny Benjamin's home address at Beckenham was on file, so he'd been in Webber's sights since early on. It was the DC's long weekend off, but with a glimmer of hope from his talk with Revenue and Customs he was prepared to spend an April day 'keeping an eye' on a tasty target.

That morning Benjamin had driven his Toyota down the A2 to Meopham, and after a couple of hours inside Dawson's done-up farmhouse he had switched to the

Jaguar and driven his boss back up the A2 to the Deptford nightclub. Another hour or so, and then he was off in the Ford, threading his way through Lewisham to Bromley, and on along the A233. Which could be leading anywhere; and Ian Webber was just switching his radio to Magic FM for the long haul when Benjamin suddenly pulled over. The cars in between braked sharply, a horn sounded, and Webber pulled out to go driving on past. *Carry on and come back* – never show yourself by pulling over behind the target when what he's probably doing is checking if he's got a tail. But as well as the sudden stop, it was where that stop had happened that surprised Webber. It was at Biggin Hill airport, used by both weekend flyers and business executive jets.

'Oh, yes?' Webber drove further on and turned in a bungalow entrance to return to where Denny Benjamin was parked. And Webber cursed: not because the guy had spotted his tail – which he hadn't – but because the Ford was dropping someone off: someone Webber hadn't seen getting into it. Had he been shielding his face behind an A to Z mapbook when this person came out of the nightclub? Or was the passenger already in the van? It was no one he knew, and it turned out not to be a man. It was a young woman in a blue-grey air hostess uniform who was walking like a model towards the airport buildings. Webber didn't fly a lot, but the uniform was not British Airways, or Easyjet, it was some private livery, topped by a perky hat with a red flash along the side. He drove on past, heading back the way they'd come, to park further along near a line of spotters at the perimeter fence, all focused on the take-offs and landings. He got out of his car and sidled over to one who was bulging the fence with his stomach.

'Nice uniforms,' Webber said, 'those cabin crew in the grey.' The woman could be seen along to their right, going into the main building.

The spotter, wearing a shiny Battle of Britain replica flying jacket, looked round at Webber. 'Wouldn't suit you. Wouldn't go with those trainers.'

Webber laughed. 'What company's that, then?'

'Red along the hat?'

'Yeah, that woman, just gone in.'

'That's Aix Airways; Biggin Hill–Marseilles twice a week.' The man pronounced the name of the south of France city in a very English way.

'Marseilles?' Webber repeated the pronunciation.

'"Aix and Pains Airlines" they call them. Not much leg-room in those Hamlets. Used to fly out of London City but couldn't afford the landing charges. A few passengers and a lot of cargo.'

'Smart-looking personnel, though.'

'Trolley-dollies.' The man shut his face tight and turned away to tune his shortwave receiver, as if this had gone far enough. He clamped his earphones tighter to his head.

'Cheers.' Webber moved away, as at that moment Denny Benjamin's Ford van headed past, back along the A233. Which Webber didn't bother to follow. *Biggin Hill–Marseilles!* Marseilles was a prime port of arrival into France for all sorts of illegal stuff from North Africa: drugs, cigarettes, immigrants – some of them girls bound for brothels in European towns and cities. So had his day paid off? Had DC Ian Webber made a real discovery, coming here to Biggin Hill? Had he got a lead that looked like fitting his theory?

Well, time and a bit more leg work would tell—

When she'd got to Cockfosters station earlier Amber had looked for a public lavatory but there wasn't one; now she knew it would be over an hour's ride on the Underground before she got to one at North Greenwich, and after that tussle with the Alsatian she could use a visit somewhere. But on her way along the road to Papendreou's house she'd passed the entrance to Trent Park – so might there be bushes in there for a girl to hide behind? It was open to the public even though a sign said it was part of Middlesex University. Now, on her way back to the station, she took a detour and followed a couple of women walking their dogs in through the park gates.

Bad luck – there were no handy bushes just inside, everywhere was too open, so Amber followed the roadway towards a signposted café – and 'TOILETS'.

'Result!' she said aloud, and headed for them. But she didn't get there – not straight away; because she first had to cross a T-junction with a wide road, and here she suddenly found herself facing a long, straight avenue – and, *knock-out!* – she'd never seen anything like this before. She stopped, her mouth open; not gaping at the long lines of tall trees but at what was growing underneath them. Everywhere she looked, as far and as wide as the park, grew swathes and swathes of daffodils, millions of them, great clusters of light yellows, and mid-yellows, and deeper yellows, a glorious sight of spring colour that made her stand and stare.

'That is *beautiful!*' It was awesome. To have come from the hatred of Papendreou's guard dog, to have churned with the anger of what that house meant to her, to have had the blood of revenge boiling inside her body – and then to come to a sight like this, where someone had planted all this peace . . . It was magic. And in a weird sort of shock, she started to cry. In her state of mental turmoil, like hearing the first kind word after a very bad time, the sight of those acres of daffodils just brought her to tears.

And one of the deep-down reasons was the sad fact that in his ten years of life Connor had never had the chance to see anything as beautiful as this.

She stood taking it all in, until her body reminded her why she'd come into the park in the first place. She turned and walked towards the toilets, which were at the side of a small area for cars. Inside, the building was swept and clean, and there was paper, and soap, hot water, and an efficient hand drier. She checked her face in the mirror – yes, they'd even provided a mirror, which wasn't cracked or scratched with glass graffiti – blinking her eyes clear of tears and dabbing at where the mascara had smudged. To be suddenly brought away from herself by a yelp of laughter, a girl first, and then other people joining in; *kind* laughter, like between friends, men and women.

'She gave it an "A"!' a girl was saying.

'That's Gammidge for you.' This was a man. 'Bung it back to her without changing a word, and she thinks her tutorial has made all the difference . . .'

Amber stretched onto her toes to look through the mesh of the window. Two boys and two girls were at a small convertible, pulling back the hood to the fresh air, one of the girls standing checking through an essay, or something.

'Not another mark on it, and she's written *"Much better"* at the bottom. With an "A".'

'Don't question it, then, Ange. Accept what Gammidge gives . . .'

They laughed, and piled into the car, students with shoulder bags and rucksacks, looking like characters in one of those films where everyone starts singing as they drive along the open road. These people had to be from the university at the other end of that long avenue through the daffodils. And as Amber came down off her toes, something that traitor Sunil Dhillon had said to her came into her mind: stuff about being a student, and the Sussex Downs, and the freedom, the friends, the mucking-about time in your life. And from nowhere came the words of a poem she'd once had to learn for a school poetry performance, about a London girl from a poor background.

"'Give me a boy till seven," they say, and I'll give you the man.
But girls like me unfortunately go quickly down the pan.'

Amber turned back from the window to face an open cubicle. So where did she belong, then? Down that pan *there*, or out of the window among the daffodils *there*?

Well, right now she didn't know. And one thing was for sure – she would only know after she'd punished the person who'd killed her Connor, and she had properly laid his soul to rest.

When she came up from the Underground at North Greenwich the first voice she heard was Sunil Dhillon's, on her voice mail. She switched the phone straight off. The little creep would only be making excuses, explaining himself, rubbish about how he'd been deliberately trying to bring the funeral incident out into the open so the police would have to follow it up. That sort of thing.

The big surprise when she got home was Matalan Man – who was standing in disguise, looking up towards the balconies of Bartram House. *Disguise?* – well, he wasn't in his suit today, but in a baseball cap and leather jacket.

'No school today?'

'Day off for Higher Education. You heard my dad. You banged-up Mr P yet?'

'Not yet.'

'You seen the *Sun*?'

'Nope.' He was walking with her towards the entrance to the flats. 'Day off.'

'Oh, this is fun time, is it?' Amber wasn't going to break step for him. She came to the entry keypad, and put her hand over it while she tapped in her personal number.

'Don't bother with secrecy, Amber – I've got the master code for all of these . . .' He waved a hand around the Barrier Estate.

'But you haven't got the code to *me*, Sunshine.' She fixed him with with a stare. 'Not till you sort who killed my Connor.'

Webber leaned his hand against the entrance wall. 'That's why I'm here this afternoon, and not looking at paintings in the National Gallery.'

'Oh, culture.' The outer door had buzzed and was ready for Amber to push: she had eighteen seconds before her tap-in was cancelled. 'So what've you come here for? Me, or my mum?'

'You, Amber.'

'Oh, yes?'

'Hajdu. Do you know anyone called Hajdu?'

'You know I do. He's in my form.' He would have checked – had she got another double-dealing 'twicer' here?

'Did Connor know him?'

'*Connor*? *My* Connor? Why would he? Hajdu doesn't live on the estate, he's a bus ride away, and Connor's years younger. *Was.*'

'I just wondered.'

Amber turned to the keypad again. 'And I wonder why you just wondered? Hajdu's a mouthy nothing: always on about guns, and knives, and violent stuff – but it's all in his crazy head. Why in hell should Connor go within a million miles of him?' She scowled at Webber. 'What is it you're getting at?'

'I'm not getting at anything, other than trying to rule out a local family from having anything to do with what happened to Connor. You've seen Alfie Walters, you jogged his memory, and he's saying now that prior to the fall he saw Connor running along the landing of Riverview as if he was being chased. Amber, I'm trying to rule *out*, not include *in*.'

Amber took a breath. 'I still know I'm right – Peter Hajdu's not for real: he thinks life's like a Playstation game.'

'Nice way of putting it.'

'Oh? Give me an "A", will you?'

But Matalan Man didn't smile. 'I'll give you an "L" for being loyal to your brother.'

'Thank you *very* much. Is that it?' Amber pushed her face nearer his. 'Have I got your permission now to go an' smoke a joint and down a bottle of Barcadi?'

'Sure. I'm off for a shower, and then a film.' He pulled his baseball cap down over his eyes, and turned, and went.

While Amber closed her eyes, and saw daffodils.

Debra was still not back home, but an hour and a half later, Lauren rang again – came straight to the point of the call.

'Amb, Half Past Yesterday – the tickets are here. Came to Dad's agent this morning.'

'Great!'

'We're in B2, Category One tickets.'

'Terrif!'

There was a long pause, unknown between Amber and Lauren. At last – 'Guess you didn't come to school on account of the *Sun*. Your dad . . .'

'Why shouldn't I come? I'm not ashamed of anything. Everyone knows he's in prison.'

'You don't fancy Midnight Express tonight?'

Amber didn't need long to think about that. 'Not in the mood for clubbing.' The friends had had some good nights up in Deptford, but that wasn't for tonight.

'Yeah. Hey – you want to come over my place? Dad's got a gig and Mum's going – and I've got Cogs an' Dogs, advance copy, High Definition.'

'OK.' Why shouldn't she go out somewhere which wasn't jumping up and down? After everything, it would be good to be a bit normal. 'What time?'

'Half seven?'

'Great.'

'See you later, Amb.'

'See you later, Lor.'

Amber switched on the local news. She'd missed the start, but as item followed item it looked as if Sunil Dhillon's reporter wasn't on that night. It was Friday, and they were down to boring items about weekend events around the region, then the football matches London clubs were playing the next day – and Dermot Mark didn't do sport. Dhillon was probably off somewhere spending the money the *Sun* had paid him for betraying Amber Long . . .

Chapter Fourteen

In her tie-waist Burberry coat – a cheap copy – Amber stood waiting for the lift. It was a twenty-minute walk to Lauren's place on the Thames riverside. The evenings were getting longer, but once the sun started going down the weather still had a touch of winter to it, so she wore her long brown boots and kept her hands in her pockets. Which was a mistake straight off. When the doors of the lift opened, two men were in it, getting out. They passed Amber, no one looking anyone else in the face, but as the doors closed, the men suddenly turned and came back at her, one of them pressing the ground floor button, the other pushing Amber against the lift wall – with her hands trapped in her pockets.

'Get off!'

The man had crimped grey hair and a face like a rock cake; his partner had blue glasses, a sleek shine to his head and a tan; and both of them wore long black coats like the coffin bearers at Connor's funeral.

'Get off me!'

'No noise, please!' Rock Cake put a black leather hand tight across her mouth. 'You choose. Someone, he wants to see you.' He sounded Eastern European, or Italian, or Greek. Amber's eyes stung with anger. 'You will not get hurt – this is a promise. You come with us, you walk to a car, you do not shout. You have a little ride, you drink some Coca-Cola, you listen to the man, and you go home.'

Now the man with blue glasses spoke, pulling a wet, smelly, hospital pad from a plastic bag in his pocket. 'Or if you want to fight I have to knock you out. Dreamy land.' He waved the pad in front of Amber's face: it smelled repulsively chemical. 'Only, a very bad head, after.'

Amber's arms were pinned tight, and breathing through a leather glove meant she couldn't speak, anyway.

'You nod OK. Or . . .'

The pad was held up nearer Amber's nose; already it smelled noxious enough to make her feel sick. She forced her head forward against the glove in a curbed nod: the last thing she wanted was to be knocked out.

'Good. We are friends.'

No, we're bloody not! Amber's mind was volcanic. Who was this man who wanted to see her? Papendreou? Or some friend of the Hajdus? Had someone seen the policeman talking to her? In the pressure of her rage she could feel blood vessels straining behind her eyes. Why should she trust these two? She knew too well that she could go quietly, and still end up floating in the Thames.

But she had no choice in what happened. She was pinioned. She couldn't scream, she couldn't fight, she couldn't run. The lift reached the ground floor and she was half-carried out. A black van was parked with its back to the flats entrance, the doors open and its engine running. Out of the building, she was shoved across a metre of concrete and lifted into the van like stolen goods; and almost before the lift doors had closed behind them, she was being driven away from Bartram House to join the Friday evening traffic through the Blackwall Tunnel.

She had never been inside such a big car. The van had pulled into a lay-by somewhere on the other side of the river, part of a new development from the looks of it – with Canary Wharf looming above her. Like before, she was out of the back of the black van in one swift lift, and put into a car which was as big as a funeral limo. And in the back of it, behind its tinted windows, sitting like some maharajah on a white leather seat, was the man whose face had been on the front of the *Sun* that morning. Dimitris Papendreou. He lifted a hand and indicated where she would sit, facing him on a similar seat – and still there was room for her legs and feet without them touching his. The other men backed away, and the car started to move, while the Greek leaned to a built-in refrigerator at his side and poured a can of Coke into a crystal glass.

'Have!' he said, nodding, not in any way to be defied. He looked smaller in the flesh than he had in Amber's mind. She'd built him up to be an ogre, but here he sat, wiping his hand from the frost off her glass with an orange silk handkerchief from his top pocket. 'Frank Sinatra memento,' he said.

Amber stared across the car. She knew about Sinatra, an icon to Lauren's dad. He'd been a hard drinker; but Mr P was sipping water.

'Orange silk handkerchief for the top pocket. Bring him luck, Sinatra said.' Papendreou nodded at his as he replaced it.

'This is abduction!' Amber shouted at him. 'Kidnap!' She could make a mess of his suit and his orange hankie if she threw this glass of Coke in his face. 'You could be doing anything to me in here!'

'With my daughter here?' Papendreou laughed – and behind Amber's head the glass panel between her and the front seats slid open. She twisted her head – to see a girl sitting beside the driver up front.

'Hi! I'm Ariadne,' the girl said – in a voice more north London than Greek. 'We're taking you back in a minute. You was going out?'

'*I was!*'

'Give us directions when we're nearer.' And she slid the panel closed.

Papendreou leaned forward. 'I want to talk, this is

all. I want to put straight some things.'

Amber faced the man again.

'You are wild with me. You do not look so beautiful on CCTV at my house when you anger my dog. You do not need to do this.'

Amber stared at him. He was relaxed, and old-uncle-looking as he took off his thick glasses and cleaned them on that stupid Sinatra handkerchief.

'You tell me why I don't need to!'

They had stopped at lights. People on the pavement stared at the limousine, but Amber knew they couldn't see in – it would be no good waving, and shouting for help.

'I did not kill your brother. I did not order your brother to be killed. It was garbage your father shouted in the funeral.'

'Oh, was it?' Amber leaned right over to thump her glass on the top of the refrigerator, which Panedreou steadied without looking at it. 'He had messages in prison. My mum had messages to give him. He had stuff to do for you – but he didn't . . .'

Papendreou tidied away the glass. 'Yes, this is true. And you know like me why he did that thing that put him in the prison. He paid me this piece of his debt. But I am a fair man, in business and in life. I have family.' He waved his hand to indicate Ariadne in the front again. 'I back off. He has lost his son in tragedy – this man does not need to be punished.' He took an iPhone from an inside pocket, tapped it. 'OK, I give orders and people do what I say. I punish when I have to punish, everybody knows this, then I do not look a big fool. But I would be happy to look a big fool if it would bring back your brother.' He leaned forward and laid four long fingers on Amber's arm. 'I make big noise for the newspaper – solicitors, such talk is expected – but you see how I do not harm you, and I swear to you I did not harm the son of Jonny Long.' He sat back, nodding, as if he was content that he had set the record straight.

Amber frowned at him, shifted on the leather seat against which the backs of her legs were sticking.

Suddenly he leaned forward, further this time, as if he might attack. Amber pressed her head back into soft leather. 'You can go to police and say I have abducted you. Now you can bring charges, and I will have to go to court. 'I have put myself in your hands tonight, to prove I am a man of honour.' He looked Amber in the eyes. 'On the life of my daughter, Miss Long, I did not have any link to your brother's death.' He sat back. 'You look at gangs, is best,' the man went on. 'Gangs, they buy stuff from dealers – cigarettes, drink, drugs – they sell on their patch. Eh? Estates like yours. So one gang is starting to sell in another territory. And what happens? Little war. Someone dies, perhaps a warning. It is in all the papers all the time.' He sat back. 'This is where you look, not at Dimitris Papendreou. Hands all clean.' He dusted his hands to show how clean.

The car was coming out of the Blackwall Tunnel again, returning to the Greenwich side. The glass panel behind Amber slid open once more and Ariadne spoke through. 'Where are we going, Amber?' She said it like an old friend.

But could you ever trust friends like these? 'Anywhere near the O_2.' Amber definitely wasn't going to be taken any closer to the river than that, not by these people.

'I told him he'd got to put you straight,' Ariadne said. 'I could've wept for you, at our gate, scared by our guard dog . . .'

And Amber had thought she'd been the scary one. 'Don't you worry about me. I'm cool.' But she was relieved when they dropped her at the O_2, from where she could walk along to Lauren's – with that black van stopping close behind Papendreou's car. She watched kids heading into the arena for a concert, who looked at the limousine as if it might be their star arriving, and gave her long stares as she got out. When the Papendreou vehicles had driven off she stood aside and tapped Lauren's number into her mobile.

'Lor?'

'Amb? Where are you?'

'On my way. Ten minutes.'

'Where've you been?'

Amber looked up at the darkening sky, and back at her boots. 'Sorry, got held up. Won't be long.' She started to run, just in case she was being followed, not sure whether or not she believed Ariadne or Mr Papendreou. What he had told her could have been the truth – or all that laying himself open could have been just a big bluff; he could have been creating a smoke screen by throwing that gangs stuff at her. But Amber knew it could well be true – because, God, didn't gangs take it out on rival gang members when they had a grudge?

Who was there to prove anything one way or the other, though? And, running along the riverside to Lauren's posh town house, she suddenly felt more alone in the world than ever.

The door to Jonny Long's cell was suddenly opened. It was five a.m., and 'wake up' time was normally six. Senior Police Officer Brighouse was at the door.

'Long?'

'What?'

'Get out of that pit an' get your stuff together.'

'What for?'

'Don' ask stupid questions. You're moving. You don't ponce around at funerals embarrassing my mates an' stay in cosy Marwood with us . . .'

'Not worried.'

'Well you won' think that where you're going.'

'Where's that?'

Frank Lodge was awake now, and rocking the bunk

with a disgruntled turn-over, away from the officer.

'Think *north*, Long. Think a long way away up north. You reckon you're hard? There's animals where you're going.' And Brighouse went.

'That'll mean loss of remission, an' all,' Lodge said. 'Longer 'fore you can get your revenge.'

'Shut up!' said Jonny Long. 'I done more at that funeral than you ever will with your pie in the sky.' And he ripped Lodge out of his bunk to thump his head on the floor before Brighouse could get back to stop the violence.

Amber came home to the flat – where she was stopped by a light in the hallway, which she had not left on, shining through the glass pane of the front door. She stood away, didn't let herself in with the key because it could be anyone in there – those Greeks, or, if she went by what Papendreou had said, some gang turning the place over. Instead, she knocked on the woodwork and backed against the balcony wall. A shape eventually crinkled through the glass – and from the hang of the head, Amber knew that her mother had turned up. With everything going on, she'd almost forgotten the woman.

''Aven't you got a key?' Debra asked, standing there in the same dress she'd worn to Connor's funeral, but so sweaty it looked as if she'd been for a swim in it.

'Just look at the state of you!' Amber pushed past

her mother, through into the kitchen. 'Where've you been?'

'Couldn't tell you, to be honest.' Debra had followed, and sat, holding her head. 'Make us a nice cup of tea, Amb . . .'

'Off drowning your sorrows? Who with? Winston? Or that man with the envelope?' Amber clattered a couple of mugs and plugged in the kettle.

'Gawd knows.' Debra groaned. 'Got a fag?'

'Don't smoke.'

Debra lifted her head, with some pain. 'What man with what envelope?' Amber saw the fog swirling behind her mother's eyes, clearing, clouding, clearing . . .

'At the Captain Cook. A black guy – just your cradle-snatching type – he came in and gave you something.'

'Did he?' More swirling. 'Oh, yeah – him. Yeah, he gave me something . . .'

'So what was it?' Amber put a mug in front of Debra, the teabag still in it – which Debra straight away started to drink.

'A few notes, that was all.'

'Why? Why would he give you money? Was there a message with it, was anything written on the envelope? Have you *got* the envelope? And the money?'

'Spent it.'

'I bet you have.'

'Paid for a couple of rounds of drinks . . .'

God, for this woman cash machines could squirt out

gin and tonics.

'So what did he say when he gave it to you? Who was it from?'

Debra put her head in her hands. 'Just it was from friends,' she rasped, deep, deep, in her throat. 'Something short like that. You know the way people hand over money.'

'I wish I did. Perhaps they had a collection round the Barrier.'

Debra tried to look intelligent. 'Yeah, that's what I thought,' she said.

Amber turned away from her and went out into the hallway, where she could see into Connor's tidy room. 'Get yourself to bed – and try to wake up sober. Then see if your mudbath of a brain can remember anything about the last couple of days. That bloke could be someone we need to know about.' She went to the bathroom to clean her face – where, looking into the mirror, she told herself she'd keep an eye out for this guy; and if she saw him she'd ask him who had donated that money.

'This Literature examination,' Mr Pewtrell said on Monday, 'it's important, give it respect. It's internal, but don't treat it lightly. We keep these scores as evidence for when we contest a grade.'

Amber liked Mr Pewtrell – never called him 'Putrid' – and she liked the books and plays they were doing in English. He had a feeling for his subject, and he would open a book as if he really couldn't wait to get to the words inside it.

'So, let's get to a possible question about *A Midsummer Night's Dream*, which came up two years ago and could come up again. In some productions of this play the parts of Theseus, King of Athens and Queen Hippolyta, are played by the same actors as those who play Oberon and Titania. Can you think why that might be?' He looked all round the form room.

'Saving money?' Leanne Standing asked. '*Bog off?*

'*Bog off?*

'B-O-G-O-F. Buy one get one free.'

Which brought a good laugh – Mr Pewtrell joining in. 'And so the language develops,' he nodded, as if making a note. 'Could be, with theatre companies strapped for cash – it's a big cast. No, think of the characters, is there something in the nature of the play that might lean towards doubling those parts?'

Amber put up her hand; not high, just a sign that she'd like to speak.

'Yes?'

'Well, it's a midsummer night's dream. So perhaps all the fairies stuff is what Theseus is dreaming about. It's like, Oberon is another side of him, a sort of, secret wish . . .'

Mr Pewtrell nodded, smiled, and quoted:

"'If we shadows have offended,

Think but this and all is mended,
That you have but slumb'red here
While these visions did appear."

'I've seen those lines of Puck spoken directly to Theseus at the end. So could we go to Greek history and look up Theseus's relationship with Hippolyta, and find parallels with Oberon's with Titania? Because Shakespeare makes sure he doesn't have Theseus and Oberon onstage at the same time – although the actor would have to go off as Oberon in Act Four and come on as Theseus in the next scene. But could we make an argument drawing out that theme?'

But Amber wasn't listening any more; because her mind had suddenly gone to that place where it constantly wandered whether she was lying awake, dreaming herself, or walking the streets and the estates of Thames Reach: she was seeing Connor, her Connor; and here in the form room with her 'Dream' notes open in front of her, right now she was suddenly seeing him as Puck: as that lively, funny, spirit, here one moment, gone the next – in his room, in hers, on the landings, up on balconies and over the roofs. He couldn't have put a girdle round the earth in forty minutes like Puck – but he could be up the church steeple in four.

She had closed her eyes. And *what* was he, that Puck? He was Oberon's servant. He did what someone else told him to do . . .

So had Connor been serving someone like that, obeying a boss? Had he been given a mobile phone as payment for something he'd done, or as a piece of equipment? Had someone been running her little brother? And if so, who was it? Who had been his lord? Because after the drama of being picked up by Papendreou, and hearing what he'd said – which could be truth or it could be lie – now, sitting here in the calm of an English lesson, Amber suddenly realised that there was a chance someone existed who had been an Oberon to her little Puck.

The same person who had turned her own life into a hellish dream . . .

Amber's dark mood wasn't lightened as she went out of the school gates that afternoon. There among a line of cars meeting year sevens, something took Amber straight back to the awful day when Connor had died – the sight of a parked van with BBC painted on its side. And walking the pavement towards her was a traitor she never wanted to meet again, except to slug in the face. Sunil Dhillon. He had a whiny look to him, his two hands held out apologetically, shaking his head like someone trying to see off a migraine.

'Amber . . .'

'Shit-face!' Amber spurted from her friends and ran for him, fists up the way her dad had taught her.

'Hey! Hey!' Sunil clearly wanted to stand his ground, but Amber got to him and didn't stop, punching at the side of his face – catching him high on his cheek-bone, swearing, kicking at his shins, clawing at his neck, till he backed off, windmilling backwards. 'I'm on TV tonight! Mind the face!' He clattered through a pavement of home-going kids, who abused him for being so clumsy; until he turned, and fumbling a handkerchief to his bleeding neck, he ran for the BBC van – while Amber aimed a kick at his calf, caught it hard, and left him hopping and limping for the near-side door.

'Don't you ever show your face near me again!' she screeched, kicking at the van's side – until its driver pulled out fast, and just missed killing a kid who was crossing the road.

'Good for you, Amb, girl!' Lauren knew all about Dhillon's treachery.

But Amber didn't feel triumphant: she stood sucking in breath, Connor and Papendreou shooting through her mind.

'What're you like when you lose your rag?' a boy asked her, keeping his distance.

'You don't need to know, kid!' Amber told him. 'You don't need to know – but this shit world is sure going to find out!'

Chapter Fifteen

Detective Superintendent Brewer had listened carefully to Ian Webber. Coming into the CID office on his own agenda – collating the routine information he needed for his monthly report to the Yard – the senior policeman took some persuading away from his task. But being a good superior he gave the DC a few minutes of his time. Which gave Webber his opportunity to tell him his suspicions about Billy Dawson's nightclub operation, leading up to spelling out his theory that it could have been Dawson's right-hand man Denny Benjamin who'd tipped off Revenue and Customs about those drugs driving up the A2 through Bexley.

'But only suspicions, yeah? On the back of a public phone box an' a black voice. Bit thin, isn't it?' Brewer's nose wrinkled.

'It is thin, sir – until we find Benjamin picking up an air hostess at Dawson's club, and dropping her off at Biggin Hill Airport, where she works for a regular airline operating between here and Marseilles. Marseilles . . .' Webber put some emphasis on the place.

Brewer scratched his neck. 'Sergeant Kwayana got a view on this?'

'Haven't told her, sir.' Webber stopped, as if deciding what to say. 'She'd pull me off it.'

'Oh?' Brewer looked out through the office window as if he was distancing himself from a dispute.

'I have got a lot on, sir.'

Brewer turned back to look at Webber's desk, heaped with papers and files. 'She's dead right, son, from the looks of it.' He pulled his slipping braces up a sloping shoulder. 'Come up with this from following Benjamin on your rest day, did you?'

'Yes, sir.'

'You reckon we owe you a day?'

'No, guv, of course not.'

DS Brewer picked up a file from Webber's tallest pile. He opened it, but wasn't reading when he said, 'OK, I'll tell you what you do. Satisfy yourself. Sort out what's going on with this Benjamin. Finish your shift tonight then sit on his tail for a couple of days – an' if he's bringing in drugs by air, let's see if we can't nail him.' Brewer lifted the same file again, and tossed it back. 'I'll square Liz about some of this.'

'Thank you, sir.'

'Let's go for the big boys. Let's sort these dregs of humanity.'

Brewer went out, whistling; while Webber went

back to his computer, to sort what he could before he signed out.

Early next morning Ian Webber came down the stairs of the house he shared with his father. It was in a small modern development between Gravesend and Rochester, at Shorne village – where through powerful binoculars Reggie Webber could look out over the Kent marshes and identify river traffic and wildlife. He made himself a strong coffee and bit at an oaty bar; he wasn't a 'full English' breakfast man like Reggie, who right now was out walking the dog. He skimmed the Times inside outwards: arts reviews and sport before he looked for news stories with south London connections, for which Kent local radio would be no good – the upside of which was that by putting a twenty-mile car journey between his work and his home life, he wasn't recognised by 'faces' in the Falstaff. He lived the life of a loner, and had never let on to the likes of DS Brewer and Liz Kwayana that his retired father had finished his career in the élite ranks of Special Branch.

It was five forty-five, and getting lighter as Reggie Webber came in through the back door and took Elsie off her lead. 'Not in the office today?' He nodded at Webber's leather jacket. 'Something going down?'

'No – I'm seeing where Denny Benjamin takes himself. Missed him yesterday. Brewer's given me time

to paint a bit of a picture.' Ian Webber shared
everything with his widower dad.

'Why don't you take the van?' Reggie suggested.
'Your man must know the Vauxhall like his mother's
eyes by now.' Between them the Webbers had the
Vauxhall and a green Ford van that Reggie used for
going birdwatching out at Cliffe.

'That's not a bad idea. He doesn't, but others do.'

'I was going to give it a birthday today – but it's nice
'n nondescript as it is.'

Ian Webber looked at his active father, losing his hair
but not his zest, who would have loved to be in the
back of that van today. In his time he'd been an
undercover officer in Northern Ireland, and he'd sat in
an armour-plated Rover beside the prime minister. He
was police top dog – and his son was determined to be
the same before he finished.

Within the hour the DC was parked a few cars along
from Denny Benjamin's flat at Beckenham. The man's
Toyota sat gaudy in the shade as the locals began
trotting for trains and buses. If anyone gave the van
a second glance, it looked as if a gardener had come to
lay a patio.

Webber had to wait a long time, but the Ford was
ideally equipped – with a green pull-down windscreen
visor that fooled the birds on Cliffe marshes. He could
sit behind that and not have to pretend to be reading
a newspaper.

179

Benjamin came out at last – which was a relief, because Webber realised he could have been down at Meopham overnight, never mind that the Toyota was parked here in London. With his 'Windies' baseball cap pulled well down Benjamin checked along the road, seemed satisfied, got into his car and drove to Deptford – stopping off for ten minutes at Oddbins in Greenwich – before arriving at the Midnight Express nightclub, where he stayed inside until half-past twelve.

Ian Webber had heard the radio news on two consecutive hourly bulletins when there was sudden activity. Denny Benjamin came out of the nightclub followed by Billy Dawson, both getting into the Jaguar. With Webber tailing at a safe distance they drove along Evelyn Street to the Angel, a smart pub restaurant overlooking the river at Rotherhithe – where they went in, and stayed.

Webber made a note of every car registration in the car park; because what was going on inside could be a 'meet', criminal networking, and who knew what the plates might tell him about who was there?

He sat and ate the sandwiches his dad had cut for him, until Dawson and Benjamin eventually came out at three o'clock, with the boss treating Rotherhithe to a resounding belch. But they weren't alone: a tall, grey-cropped man in a sports jacket and jeans came out with them, to brief farewells, no smiles. Unfortunately, the man hung about and made a long mobile phone call facing out over the Thames – while Benjamin drove Dawson away in the Jaguar. Now Webber had to make a decision. He couldn't tail both cars: and he couldn't wait to see which of the parked cars the third man got into, not if he was to keep tabs on the Jag. OK, he might assume that Dawson was going back to Midnight Express, but this could be the day when he didn't – and he could picture Brewer's face, reading his report. He shouldn't make assumptions – Reggie wouldn't – but Webber would still bet his pension that this third man had *Aix Airways pilot* sewn into the label of his jacket.

His quick decision made, Webber went with the Jaguar back to Deptford and another long, long, wait, during which he gradually bettered his position on the parking meters along Church Street. Fortunately, Reggie had thought of everything, and as well as Evian water and wine gums in the glove compartment, there was a funnel and an empty bottle under the passenger seat, so Webber had no need to show himself to the wildlife.

It was boring, but this was the sort of boring that can pay off: anything might happen at the end of a long wait – or nothing. With Benjamin's Toyota here and not parked in Meopham, if he drove his boss home in the Jaguar he might have to sleep the night down there. Or Dawson could be staying overnight in London. So Webber creased himself into his father's shape and sat it out – until a surprise tap on his window told him that he'd lost it for a few minutes. Standing there was a traffic warden, pointing at the time about to run out on the meter.

Webber lowered the window. 'Cheers. I'll see to it.'

'Can't do that, sir. You can go away, if you're quick. I got to book you if you stop; feedin' the meter's an off-ence.' He was a young Somali, hitching his ticket-printing machine.

Webber knew that by the time he'd gone right round the Deptford one-way system, he wouldn't get back to this good spot with its prime view of the Jaguar, the Toyota, and the club entrance. So he fished out a pound coin and his warrant card, and offered them up to the traffic warden. 'Put this in for us, will you?'

The Somali's eyes screwed at the ID, then along to Midnight Express, and with a quick look up and down the street he did something to the meter with a key. 'Groaty place,' he said – but like a good undercover man himself he put his head in through the window to speak. 'Some people don' come here for dancing, not even if their feet's on fire. Cer-tain nights.'

'No?' With enough support from Liz Kwayana Webber might have known all this, and these people's identities. 'Put any names to them, can you?'

The traffic warden stared at him. 'I'm not tellin' you, man, even if I can.'

Webber started to raise his window.

'Esceptin' – I will tell you one. No big name, this.'

Webber twisted to face him.

'Filthy little scum . . .'

'Yeah?'

'He cut my brethren. He en-joyed it.' A spit on the pavement. 'All of them call him Trev.'

'Trev?'

'Uh-huh. Tre-vor Benjamin.'

'*Trevor* Benjamin? Not . . .'

'Not that Denzel. This is the little brother. An' big trouble.'

'Ah. Long streaked hair, mixed race?'

'You got him.'

But Webber didn't get to ask any more questions because the warden suddenly slapped the van roof and walked on to check the next meter.

Webber wound up the window and spoke the name he'd just heard into his BlackBerry; and with it the number on the traffic warden's lapel. And hours later, at one a.m., when Denny Benjamin drove Dawson down the A2 in the Jaguar, Webber tailed them only as far as their Meopham turn-off, where he carried on home, and spent another couple of hours on a secure local government internet site, coming up with an address for Trevor Benjamin.

Which he wasn't totally surprised to find had him living in Jimmy Seed house, on the Barrier Estate.

And he only just didn't wake up Reggie to tell him his result.

Chapter Sixteen

It should have been great. Amber had thought how great it was going to be ever since she'd first known three weeks ago that Half Past Yesterday was going to play the O_2: which was what spoiled it all for her now, because seconds after Lauren had phoned her, she'd run into Connor's bedroom to tell him. And in a manic mickey-take he'd jumped onto his bed and bounced, and air-guitared and wailed – bouncing so high that the bed crashed under him, leaving the two of them racing to fix it before he got a clout from Debra.

Amber tried to blank that from her head, but all she could think of this night of the concert was that first joy at knowing she was going to see Half Past Yesterday live – with Connor's contorted face, screeching *half-past, quarter-to, quarter-past, arse-blast!* No matter what she did, little Connor was hanging over her – her poor, dear, Connor – and she knew that when Half Past Yesterday leapt around on stage, all she would see was her brother going mad on his bed: Puck on acid.

'This is going to be soooo good!' As they rode the escalator to the arena entrance Lauren held up her ticket like a visa to a golden land. While Amber wished she'd lost hers.

It started with searchlights, wide, bright rods of light tinting every head in the audience, sweeping and swirling across the sudden dark. The screeching and the whooping and the uplift of heads and hands and arms almost climaxed the show before it began: but when a sudden explosion of amplified chords vibrated every backbone, up came the stage lights, and there in a dazzle was Half Past Yesterday, beating out 'We're Here!' – the sound nuclear. Amber thought she'd never hear anything as loud as the assault of the music and twenty thousand screams. Si Rowntree started loud and exuberant, leaning into the microphone; Ricky Grass flashed his sticks to hit hell out of two snares, Wen Feathers looked like melting her Gibson guitar; and 'Glor' Lovell studied his bass like a hypnotist; while three desks of strings might just as well have mimed, because set in a row behind the band was a line of brass that blew so hard the blast could be felt in row Z. No one in the arena was sitting: seats were where people stuffed their coats and stamped. It was stupendous, an out-of-body three minutes that could never be reproduced any other way: being there was the only true experience.

Throughout which Amber was somewhere else. Standing staring at the stage, she was in Connor's chaotic bedroom, shaking with laughter on the floor while her brother sat on her back, trying to push a bent bolt through a hole in the bed frame. And as Lauren looked round at her contorted face streaming with tears, hugging her tight because tonight was so fantastic, Amber shouted something for the whole world to hear.

'I bloody loved him!'

'He's fantastic!' Lauren shouted back, misunderstanding.

Favourite song followed favourite song, while Amber stood and cried her emotion out into the arena: a wail of despair and anger among the ecstasy.

Which was when Amber suddenly froze. As the audience jumped and danced a space opened a metre along from her – and what were those? Black leather boots, with a pull-up tag at the back snagging a leg of drainpipe trouser – giving off a flash of fancy laces: cross-over tied laces, blue in the left boot, red in the right. *You go looking for something and you don't find it. You're not looking, and what comes up and hits you?* Suddenly short of breath, Amber ducked along to the person wearing them, a boy about her own age or a bit older, a good-looking Afro-Caribbean with short-spiked gelled hair, wearing a Half Past Yesterday T-shirt, and a diamond stud in one ear. Someone she had definitely seen before. She timed his jumps to tap him hard on the shoulder. He turned and smiled; then frowned as he seemed to register who this was.

'You know who I am, don't you?' she said.

For a second he looked as if he might deny it. 'Sure. You was at your bro's fun'ral.'

'And so were you, right inside.'

'Yeah.' He stopped moving, everyone around them still jumping to the music, stared at her, like, *can I help you?*

'You just like funerals, do you?' Amber asked. 'Else, why were you there? Not selling Playstations cheap in your PlayCo shirt?'

Half Past Yesterday finished the song and Si Rowntree grabbed the microphone to tell everyone how great it was to be at the O_2. Every sentence got a whoop, but the place was quieter now than before.

'He was a mate,' the boy said.

'A mate? He was ten!'

PlayCo Boy didn't want all this; he wanted to brush Amber off, every fidget of his body said so. But there was no way he'd lose her – and he seemed to know it. 'He was brethren,' he said into her ear, and turned away to end the matter.

Brethren! Connor had been in a gang! Her little loner brother had belonged to something all along. But Amber had suspected something like that, hadn't she? Inside. she had. And for how long? From the time she'd gone to meet traitor Dhillon in Greenwich Park? So was this guy here her brother's Oberon?

'Gang brethren!' she said.

'You got it.'

'Barrier Crew?'

'I said, "You got it".'

But Amber wanted it on the line, the whole thing confirmed and every word understood between them. 'You're telling me Connor Long was Barrier Crew?'

Si Rowntree came away from the microphone and clicked his fingers to a deafening roar of anticipation.

'Doing what?' Amber shouted at the side of the boy's head. 'Connor wasn't a fighter, didn't beef. He wasn't *into* anything.'

On keyboard now, Si Rowntree played the opening chords of 'No Way to Go', Wen Feathers' solo hit, and the place erupted again – shouting, waving, jumping – and PlayCo boy beside Amber tried his best to jump away from her. But she'd got her fingers stuck into his belt; she was attached to him.

'What did Connor *do*?' she shouted.

He spun on her, looked down at her hold on his belt – as if worried this was a knife he could feel – was she going to stab him?

'He was a *younger*,' he put his face close to her to growl. 'He watched the corners.'

' "Watched the corners"? What corners?' *What was this guy on about? What corners had Connor watched?*

'He was look-out.' But the boy had to know that wasn't enough. He added, 'Looking out for the Romas coming in our ends.'

'No way to go for a girl like me,
No way to go I can see . . .' Wen Feathers hushed it
deep into her microphone.

'That's why he had a mobile phone,' Amber said.
'T-mobile.'

'You're not wrong.'

'Except if you give me a road I can take
That leads somewhere sunny, and free.'

Amber was trying to get her head round this when
a sudden blinding explosion sent a million glittering
coils of red foil up and out into the arena – the whole
place jumping this way, then that, followed by another
explosion in yellow bursting up on the other side of the
stage. And when Amber's eyes had blinked themselves
into seeing again, PlayCo Boy had gone – leaving her
standing there in the rocking crowd, separated from
everyone else by what she'd just been told.

Now she knew for sure why Connor had died. It had
been gang murder. And worse – or better – she knew
who had done it: not the Somali Charlton Boyz but the
Romas he'd been looking out for, what the Crew saw as
enemy, trying to move into the Barrier Estate to sell
their own people's drugs. Papendreou had been right.
Now she had got to start looking for someone local.
The Roma she was targeting for revenge.

Obsessed with what she'd been told at the O_2 the
night before, Amber came home from Thames Reach

Academy having all day looked at faces, listened to voices, seen everyone in the place as a member of some gang or other; and in her obsession she had pictured how she was going to avenge Barrier Crew Connor Long. It was going to be with a knife. A knife was easy, she didn't need to buy one; they had a long, sharp, vegetable knife in the kitchen drawer which would fit diagonally into her shoulder bag.

But on her way into the flat to check they still had it, what was going on? There were female voices in the front room. Who was this strange woman with her mother? Was it one of the aunts? Surely it wasn't Dawn Feldman again . . .?

Amber wanted to get into the kitchen, but as she slid along the corridor two words flew out at her: 'commotion' and 'funeral'. She changed her mind and went into the front room.

A woman in a lilac trouser suit was sitting in an armchair. She had to be around Debra's age but her Elizabeth Arden face seemed ten years younger than her mother's. The woman stood up to shake Amber's hand.

'I'm –'

'This lady's from the Co-op funeral service . . .' Debra said from the settee.

'Oh, yes?' Amber looked from one woman to the other, trying to read expressions. Were the Co-op going to charge extra for what Jonny Long had done in the chapel?

'I've come to apologise to your mother on behalf of Co-operative Funerals,' the woman said, sitting again.

Amber frowned.

'One of their men –' Debra began, smokily.

'One of our employees breached your client trust in us, and violated the discretion our service prides itself upon . . .'

Amber twisted her mouth. What had this employee done – stolen some of Connor's flowers?

Debra told her. 'He was waiting ready to usher us out of the door at the front, an' he was close-to when your dad was carryin' on – an' he phoned the Sun about it.'

A sudden ice hit Amber, she felt dizzy, actually rocked. 'Who did?' she managed to ask.

'One of our pall-bearers . . .'

'*Shit!*'

'He heard the name,' Debra went on. 'He sold 'em the story.'

'Certainly not up to our professional standard. You'll be relieved to know he has been dismissed from the service . . .'

Amber heard herself snort. She had put the blame for the Papendreou story on Sunil Dhillon. She had sworn at him, and punched and scratched him – badly – and then she'd kicked a dent in a BBC van.

'Oh, no!' She left the funeral woman to Debra, rushed along to her room and threw herself onto the bed. What sort of idiot had she been? Sunil Dhillon carried

191

the mark of her claws *but he hadn't been the one who'd betrayed her*, it wasn't him who'd made a quick buck out of Connor's funeral. He talked about trust, but Amber Long hadn't shown any. She grabbed at her mobile phone and called his number, checking the time: 16:53. But he'd be doing his job somewhere with his phone switched off. *'You are through to the voicemail of Sunil Dhillon. Please leave your message after the tone . . .'* She ended the call. She had rung him without thinking what she'd say; but a voicemail message was different; talking to no one made you plan it.

Immediately, her phone rang.

'Amber, it's Sunil – you rang me . . .'

'Yes. I did. Yes.'

'I'm in Oxford Street.'

'Listen – I was *so* wrong . . .'

'Mark's just wrapped an interview . . .'

Amber was somehow keeping from crying. 'How's your neck?'

'It's still holding my head off my shoulders . . .'

'Sunil—'

'Don't say anything. *I* know – and *you* know. Here – could you get to Alexandra Palace tonight?'

'What time?'

'Half past six?'

'I s'pose so.' Amber had heard of Alexandra Palace, bands did concerts there, but she hadn't got the first idea where it was.

'Part of my training – I'm being lent to Arts and Science. They're doing a recce at the dress rehearsal of the *Ramayana*, a piece for London Culture. We've got press access . . .'

'A "recce"?'

'Reconaissance. Sussing it out.'

'Is it on the Underground? What's the nearest tube station?'

She heard the rustle of paper. 'Wood Green, Piccadilly line. You go, North Greenwich to Green Park on the Jubilee, and change to the Piccadilly. Ring me from Wood Green station, and I'll pick you up.'

'OK.' Amber looked at the time. She could get to Wood Green by half past six. 'Yeah, I'll be there.'

'And no apologies – is that a promise?'

'What's the *Ramayana*?' Amber evaded. 'I've heard of it, but—'

'Wait and see. Around half-six at Wood Green, then?'

'Around half-six.'

'*And no apologies!*'

He hung up. Of course she was going to apologise for being such a stupid, jumping-to-conclusions idiot.

Either that, or she'd have to kiss him better.

Sunil came in a black cab – while Amber was looking for his scooter.

'Amber! Here!'

She dodged across the pavement and took the hand

hanging out of the taxi. He was smiling at her, but she couldn't smile back when she saw his neck – where his injury was there for the world to see, three deep scratches only slightly masked by concealer.

'Thanks for coming.'

'Thanks for the invite.' She clambered in, and as the taxi pulled away she leaned across and kissed him on the cheek. 'It was one of the coffin bearers,' she said. 'The funeral manager came to say sorry to Debra.'

'She sacked him,' Sunil confirmed. 'I went to see her after I got on to a mate on the *Sun* – he gave me a good clue to where the story had come from.'

'Oh, God...' Amber felt terrible all over again; Sunil was such a nice bloke, he'd treated her really decently, right from the beginning over Connor's photograph.

'Leave it!' he said, as they stop-started through the traffic.

'I've got some news,' she told him.

'What's that?'

'I've found out Connor was Barrier Crew. He was a "younger", watching the corners.'

'Is that a look-out?'

'It's where his climbing came in, I reckon. Up high. He had to spot Romas coming onto Crew ends to sell their drugs...'

Sunil nodded very slightly, nothing *I-told-you-so* – although he had, way back in Greenwich Park.

'Some south London Romanian gang.' She squared

towards him, and just about kept her voice steady. 'It was them that killed my Connor . . .'

The taxi took a swift swerve around a car – and slid Sunil into her, along the leather seat. 'Sorry.' He edged away, but not too quickly. 'Do you *know* this – I mean, about the Romanians?'

'It's got to be! Who else would do it? He had a mobile phone the Crew gave him, and he had to use it to finger Romas. I met a Crew and he told me. Now, if that lot found out what he was doing . . .'

'Which would tally. Putting down a marker. The day Connor died was the first day of the trial that sent a Romanian drug importer to prison for ten years.'

Amber's back stiffened. 'So . . . what happened to Connor . . . wasn't them stopping him: it was one gang paying the other one back . . .'

'If it was Barrier Crew that got the Romanian caught . . .'

'*If?*'

'Well, it's got to be "if" till we're sure, hasn't it? It's the sort of stuff lawyers check all the time at the BBC. I'll give Ian Webber a ring, do a bit of digging with CID.'

Amber drew a long, deep, breath. Sunil was right, you had to be sure. By going on half facts she might already have done something to Papendreou – as well as actually assaulting this man here. 'Don't say too much,' she told him. Because when she *was* sure – God, someone was going to pay for it!

And she was still thinking that, and clutching the shoulder bag that would soon have a knife in it, as the taxi took them through the gates of Alexandra Park, and up the hill towards the palace.

Chapter Seventeen

Amber felt like a professional. Sunil introduced her to Krishna Roy, the BBC producer from London Culture, and to the note-taking director and the senior camera operator who would all be there the following night. Straight off, Sunil gave her a BBC memo pad and asked her to make a note of any part of the story that puzzled her. Her queries would help them make things clear for viewers.

'We're not covering the whole caboosh,' he said, 'it's not an OB of the entire thing; but we want to give the essence . . .'

The *Ramayana* was being performed in the Alexandra Palace ice rink, its surface covered by flooring. All the seating ran along one side, facing a spectacular backdrop from one end of the rink to the other – of bright mountains, exotic trees, leaping monkeys, and mythical Indian figures.

'That's fantastic!' Amber said as the lights went up on it.

'Except we can't get the whole thing into one shot,' moaned Ron the cameraman – the same way as the others included her in talk about 'get-in' times, and the deadline for a 'wrap', just as if she were one of the team. They were moving about to get different angles of the show, easy because there was no audience, just the *Ramayana* director, two people on 'follow' spots, and the sound and electrics. And it was a proud moment for Amber when a *Ramayana* assistant came up to ask her if the BBC minded if they 'went up' in about fifteen minutes: they were running a bit late.

Already Amber was feeling a different person. 'OK,' she said – meaning she was about to go and tell Sunil what she'd been asked – but the girl went away before Amber could get out of her seat; her response had been taken as the nod. With Sunil in a huddle with the director, Amber had to tell Krishna Roy.

'That's fine,' Krishna said, turning away to something else; which made Amber really feel one of them.

Eventually the house lights dimmed, silence fell, and the 'Ramayana' began. And by now Amber knew what this was all about. It was the 'Rama and Sita' story she'd heard in primary school – a prince and princess in love up against the wickedness of the demon Ravena with his ten heads and twenty arms, who was madly in love with Sita: good and evil to be acted out before her. But this show turned out to be so much more than seeing the story on a normal stage: it filled the whole of the rink with a hundred performers – dancers, acrobats, actors and singers, with local schoolchildren inside huge tissue-paper gods and animals – in solemn procession and joyful dance at the spectacular meeting of Rama and Sita.

'They made those creatures at their schools,' Sunil said. 'Tissue paper and gaffer tape! Let's hope they last till tomorrow.' His serious eyes said that this was from his family's culture, and a slight click in his throat at the betrothal of Rama and Sita told Amber how much pride this gave him.

> 'Softly came the sweet-eyed Sita, bridal blush upon her brow,
> Rama in his manly beauty came to take the sacred vow.'

Glancing back at him, Amber smiled: he looked like a kid who'd just let you taste his own cooking.

The children came back later as fearsome monsters and demons fighting in the jungle, almost too realistic in the hand-to-hand stuff.

Amber opened her own programme notes – and read how the cast had been trained by fight directors in their schools. 'We never had any of this!' she told Sunil. But she wasn't thinking about herself. It was Connor who was in her head, and for the next ninety minutes she couldn't, and wouldn't, lose the thought of him: of how he would have lapped up school if this had been on offer. And when Hanuman came on, undoubtedly the most 'Connor' of all was that magical monkey, Rama's loyal disciple and son of the Wind God. It was a startling performance by a marvellous actor and dancer high above the rink – with wires for his flying, but none that Amber could see for his climbing and vaulting. He commanded the whole space with his impossible feats, skipping up ropes and bouncing off springboards to leap high above people's heads. And when Ravena torched his tail and the scenery turned red with fire everyone cheered like first night as he scampered and swung, spiralled and flew around the rink. *Just like Connor could have done, if he'd grown older and had the training!* Amber was so filled with Connor that she made hardly any notes – just one small confusion when Ravena first appeared: is *this a ten-headed demon, or ten separate demons? – get it together, guys!* Amber put the memo pad in her shoulder bag; but it wasn't a night for souvenirs. It was a night for the greatest throat-lumping sadness since Half Past Yesterday – regret, jealousy, at the sort of thing that might have been for Connor Long if he hadn't got caught up in a gang, and another gang hadn't murdered him.

And after they'd gone back to Television Centre in a BBC taxi, and Sunil had collected his scooter and two helmets to take Amber home, what she carried to bed with her wasn't the sight of Sunil's eyes as he didn't kiss her goodnight – looking as if he might – but an image of 'Hanuman' Connor, flying high without wires between the tower blocks of the Barrier Estate.

It was a Dawn Feldman day. For Amber there was beginning to be something special about her Liberal Studies sessions. Exams, qualifications, employers and the future were never mentioned by the deputy head: she would go on about them at other times, but these sessions – never *lessons* – were all about the students themselves and how they could get through their own lives. And when Mrs Feldman walked out at the end of a session she always left Amber in an upbeat mood, seeing things differently from the ways she had before.

For about five minutes. Then the fact of being Amber Long of Thames Reach kicked back in, a council estate girl on the hunt for her brother's killer – for whom revenge was the only real reason for getting out of bed.

But in a weird way the session that day gave Amber's hunt a push in a useful direction. Dawn Feldman started off with, 'I want to tell you something a woman said to me last night.' She took in each of them, round the room. 'A retired person I met at a party. I asked her where she lived: and she said, "I live in luxury in Hackney."' The teacher nodded her head on the words as she repeated them slower. '"I live in luxury in Hackney."' She gave a look Amber's way. 'Now, Mayfair, there I believe you could live in luxury. Or in a penthouse in St Katharine's Dock or Limehouse. But, come on, Hackney!?'

Amber was frowning. Where this was going?

Dawn Feldman told them. 'I must have pulled a face when she said it. Then the woman said, "Well, isn't clean running water luxury? A hell of a lot of the world hasn't got it."'

Some faces in the form room were screwed up, puzzled; others were turning, ready for talk.

Mrs Feldman rolled her shoulders; she was getting into wrestling mode. 'So you tell me – what's normal to you but a luxury to others in the world? Because I think there's lots.'

'Nothin' in Mubende,' Freddie Kisembo said. 'But up country Uganda we c'lect rain in plastics.'

'Same for us,' Peter Hajdu sneered, 'an we're not "up anywhere", man – we're in the city pits.'

'Where's that?' Mrs Feldman asked.

'Bucuresti,' Hajdu said. 'Romania.'

Amber's knee jolted up hard under the table, and it hurt. She'd never thought enough about Hajdu to worry about where the creep came from, but that had to be why Matalan Man had asked her about him. Why hadn't him being Romanian come into her head before: was it because it hadn't been important until she'd listened to PlayCo Boy? But was it just possible the police thought Hajdu could be a Roma gang member, and one of the Barrier Crew's enemies? Suddenly she couldn't wait to shove some questions at him: at the least she might find out something about his lot. She couldn't wait for the session to end. And when it did, she grabbed Lauren and Mandy and Oki and pulled them into the furthest corner of the locker lobby.

'What?'

'What?'

'*Hajdu!* Amber said.

'Bless you!'

'Peter Hajdu—' she persisted.

'What about him?'

'He's a Roma!'

'Yeah, from *Bucuresti*, in his vestie!'

Amber pulled them beyond the swing of an empty locker door. 'I've found out. It's the Romas killed my Connor ...'

'Sweet Jesus!'

'Could never be that stupid Peter Hajdu,' Oki said. 'He's all wishy mouth, no more'n that!'

Amber looked at them all, eyes alight. 'Listen,' she growled, 'we're going to find out what the little creep knows!'

'Yeah?'

'Are we?'

'Right on, Amb – why not!?'

'Come with me!' Amber was thinking of the best place for jumping Peter Hajdu, and she hadn't much doubt: the old junior school kiss-chase prison for boys – the girls' lavatories. These were next to the boys' lavatories along the lower landing between the school hall and the year eleven form rooms. And after a few terse words of planning during assembly, it was all so easy. It showed Amber how simple a hit can be when the victim's on another planet but *you* know you're going to strike – the way it probably happened with Connor's murder.

Peter Hajdu wasn't popular, he was a loner with the taint of someone who didn't even like himself; so he didn't jaunt the corridor with a crowd of others – he came slinking along against the wall like a gunman with his back covered, past the open door of the girls' lavatories; when, suddenly, 'Hajdu!' Amber beckoned from inside. He turned his head for a vital second – and 'In! In!' – the ambushing trio attacked across the corridor and pushed him into the lavatory. Amber yanked at his arm, Oki dead-legged him from behind, and inside ten seconds he was on the floor, face down, one sitting on his back, and two others pinning a calf each, his arm up his back in Amber's grip.

'Get off! What the—?'

'Shut it, Hajdu!'

Amber pushed his arm further up his back, leaned to his face. 'Hajdu – are you doing drugs on the Barrier?'

'Wha?' Peter Hajdu spasmed in an attempt to get up – but failed.

'Some of your Romas are doing drugs on the Barrier. Who is it, arsehole?'

Hajdu couldn't have mistaken or misheard. The question was shouted loudly into his face by an Amber no one had ever seen before. Today she was the violent Jonny Long's daughter. '*Eh?*' She gave his arm another push, just short of breaking it.

'Don' dirty your 'ands – 'e's nothin'!' This voice suddenly came from behind them. A year ten girl had followed them in from the corridor. 'Saw you jump him. Leave him. He's nothing. It's his brother you want when you want something.'

'What?' Amber eased her grip slightly; Oki lifted herself a fraction off Hajdu's back.

'In case you ever wanta know.' The girl was big-busted and short-skirted. '*Alex* Hajdu – he's the one: gets down the O_2 bars, an' round Thamesmead Town, an' over Plumstead Common. Anything you want.' She waved an arm at Peter Hajdu. 'Useless little ponce, this one.'

Amber and her friends got off him, Hajdu's face was screwed up with defeat and hatred. 'You just listen out for my silencer!' he warned Amber. 'I'll waste you one night.'

'Watch your mouth, Hajdu. You're not off *my* hit list yet.' And she pushed him out of the door.

'So. Alex Hajdu.' Amber looked at her friends. 'I wonder where he lives? Somewhere along the road to Woolwich . . . ?'

'I'll find out for you,' Mandy offered. She was the

tallest of the four, auburn-haired and quietly elegant. 'I'll use my female charm . . .'

The girls were sorting themselves out after their scramble on the floor. Amber stood and faced them. 'Anyhow, that was one good operation, whatever Hajdu we're talking,' she said. 'Cheers.' They were real mates, she thought: among all the rubbish of her life right now she was blessed with some loyal and decent friends.

Which, of course – her thoughts ran on – could be exactly the reason why Connor had chosen to have Barrier brethren: the poor, dead little blighter.

Ian Webber checked out of the Thames Reach CID office, getting the OK from Liz Kwayana to interview a prosecution witness in the flasher case. But his drive to the witness in Welling took him past a small shut-down police station in Wickham Lane – now used by the Community Police service, whose officers work on the estates and in local primary and secondary schools.

In particular, Webber wanted to find out more about Denny Benjamin's younger brother Trevor, who got into Midnight Express, and according to that traffic warden was handy with a knife.

Police Constable Bywater sat back in the untidy office. Computer monitors helped light the dim room, and a faulty neon tube buzzed overhead. 'Trevor? That little creep? Lives on the Barrier Estate, runs the Barrier Crew. Thinks of himself as the main man this side of the river.' Bywater was large, older than Webber and razored bald – he'd be an imposing figure standing at the front of a classroom.

'Got anything on him?' Webber was sitting across from Bywater on another side of the big table that filled the office.

'We've tried, but the kids are too scared to speak out. He does the usual stuff – initiates them the way they do, tells them to cut someone, or nick a mobile off another gang – and then they're his: in for life. But you pick up a Crew boy and he's never heard of Trevor Benjamin.'

Webber nodded. 'We ought to get together more,' he said. 'We're working on stuff with his brother.'

Bywater shook his head. 'Yeah, I can see that, on some levels. But if we're gaining confidence in the schools, talking to kids about knife crime, warning them off the gang culture, why would we want them thinking we're going to tell their stuff to CID?' He leaned towards Webber across the corner of the table. 'We've got to be their friends, not the Stasi.'

An officer at the end of the table laughed over the top of his monitor. 'You're talking to friendly Uncle Colin, there – and I'm Uncle Mick.'

'What have you got, then?' Bywater asked.

There was a long pause before Webber replied. 'Because he didn't go to school you might not have met a kid who fell from a balcony of Riverview House . . .'

'Oh, we know about him. Connor someone.'

'Connor Long. And a contact of mine tells me he was Barrier Crew.'

'Was he? Well, once Mr Benjamin had got his hands on him, he'd have had to be loyal. One minute the kids are hanging about in the underpasses, riding bikes too small, and tagging, just being together – then suddenly Benjamin wants them for other stuff: watching for when people go out then picking their locks, breaking into cars. There's still a lot of cheap cash around for electronic stuff.'

'Died in the cause then, young Connor,' Uncle Mick put in, without looking up from his computer. 'Probably on some job for Trevor.'

'Yes, probably something like that.' Webber got up to go. 'Anyhow, thanks for your time.'

Chapter Eighteen

Ian Webber was at the entrance to Amber's flats again, in a suit this time

'Caught any murderers today?' she asked.

'Not a lot.'

She had mixed feelings when she was talking to the police. As sure as hell was hot she wanted Connor's killer caught – but what punishment would he get if this Webber found him? Probably no more than double the sentence her dad had got, and if Jonny Long didn't behave himself, and Connor's killer did, there wouldn't be a lot of difference in the time they served.

'Don't go wanting him for yourself,' Webber warned.

God, was her mind that easy to read?

'Revenge is—'

'Wild justice, yeah. I've been told.'

Now she had surprised him; he gave her a nod like a teacher's tick.

'So what d'you want?' she asked.

'It's just something quick.' He glanced at his watch and looked around in a confidential way. 'A character called Trevor Benjamin was seen coming out of the

Captain Cook, the day of Connor's funeral.'

'Was he?' Amber genuinely didn't follow.

'It was when your family and friends were having a wake . . .'

'The post-mortem piss-up. What did he look like?'

'Mixed race, early twenties, tall, longish hair straightened and streaked.'

Amber knew the man he meant. Her face must have shown it.

'You saw him?'

'Dead straight, he was. Gave my mother something in a packet, and went.' Amber reckoned the policeman knew more than he was letting on; so she'd give him something to keep his suspicious mind quiet. 'Turned out to be some cash – don't know how much. So this Trevor What's-his-name has got to be Crew, because Connor was.' Which wouldn't be surprising to him: she'd told Sunil to do some digging with CID.

'Why would he give her money?'

Amber shrugged. 'Dunno. Some sort of Crew solidarity, I suppose – against the Hajdus of this world. Like a pension pay-off; like, we'll see you right . . .' *Damn!* She was so stupid, letting out a name: the name he'd used on her before. The pair stared at one another. Oh, God! Why had she opened her big mouth too wide and said "Hajdu"? Now this man would reckon he was figuring it right – that Connor had been killed by another gang; and she'd confirmed the name of Hajdu.

When she wanted that low-life for herself.

'Cheers,' Ian Webber suddenly said; and within seconds he was gone; leaving Amber with the same uncomfortable feeling she had when she'd just spent too much in a short time. Except, today she hadn't thrown holiday job pay around, it had been vital information.

Webber knew that as a name Hajdu was no Smith or Patel; and with Alexandru in front of it there was still only the one on Metropolitan Police files. Ian Webber had already tried to tail him and had failed; now, with what Amber Long had let out, he was having another go at getting close. Hajdu's name was on the police computer following an arrest and subsequent brief appearance at West End Central magistrates' court back in February, getting a fifty-pound fine for contravening a Westminster City Council bylaw for 'obstructing the general public by being in possession of, and displaying, portable advertising equipment contrary to . . . etc., etc.' So he was a 'sandwich board' man, one of those sad figures who spend their days pointing large wooden signs towards golf sales, cafés, or handbag shops. Webber went deeper into the pages and called up the facts of the case: which were that in Oxford Street in the West End of London, on 17th February that year, Alexandru Hajdu had been arrested for holding a sign that pointed to a theatre ticket agency, 'Best Seatz', owned by a Mr Radu Noica, of

Balderton Street. Webber gave a brief nod to the screen. Radu Noica was a Romanian name, and so was Alexandru Hajdu, and so was Andrei Basescu, the drugs courier. With a satisfied look on his face he printed this out, and put in a call to PC Allman at West End Central who'd made the arrest; and with great good luck he found him on duty in the station.

Both of them being constables 'in the job', Webber and Allman were soon onto first names, Ian and Alan.

'I'm interested in the Alexandru Hajdu you nicked for illegal advertising on 17th February. I'm watching him for something else; drug-dealing. Alan – what's this Radu Noica ticket agency he works for? All Romanians, are they?'

Alan Allman coughed, but it was as if his hand was over his phone, not over his mouth. 'We can't get anything to stick Noica with, not yet, he's boxing very clever, but we're dead sure he's importing ... We'll get him sooner or later.'

Which wouldn't be for importing West End musicals. 'Well, you never know, Alan – Alex Hajdu might be the way in to him. He lives down this way, I'm keeping tabs – I'll let you know if I get close. I've got a theory I'm going to run past my guv'nor. If he gives me more time on this I'll come back to you.'

'Appreciated, Ian.'

The call ended there. Ian Webber sat and thought for a bit. He was due at Thames Reach Magistrates' Court at two o'clock to present police evidence against the Blackheath 'flasher': but he just had time to drop in on DS Brewer, on the off-chance.

And he was twice lucky: the man was in his office. 'Just to let you know, sir, I'm putting together a bit of a picture on the Benjamin-Dawson front.'

Brewer looked up at him, which was permission to proceed.

'I can't substantiate a thing, but this is a strong possible . . .'

'Spill it.' Webber wasn't invited to sit, which made giving a theory without any evidence more difficult – standing there almost to attention.

'The Romanians – the network Andrei Basescu went down for at Stone Marsh Crown Court – they've been importing class A drugs through the Dartford container terminal for months. Billy Dawson, helped by Denny Benjamin, could well be importing drugs by air through Biggin Hill. So they're not in each other's way, getting the stuff in. But there's some beef between them.'

'Could be. Carry on.'

'Each outfit supplies its own territories – what the estate gangs call their "ends": the Romanians, I don't know where, probably north of the river; Billy Dawson around here. Then, for whatever reason – probably just expanding an empire – the Romanians start muscling in on Dawson's patch . . .'

'Which is where, precisely?'

'Can't be precise, sir – but, Thamesmead, Woolwich, north Kent, the riverside estates. So Denny Benjamin, on behalf of Dawson, fingers the Romanians. It was an Afro-Caribbean voice on the tip-off, made from a phone very near to Dawson's nightclub.'

'And then the Revenue and Customs roadblock pulls their delivery car . . .'

'Yes, sir.'

'So that's the Dartford supply route to the Romanians shut down. But assuming they don't know about the Biggin Hill route, they can't play tit-for-tat . . .'

'*We* don't know about Biggin Hill yet, sir.'

'Webber – none of this is hard evidence. I'm playing your game, son. So where are you now?'

'At the bottom of the pyramid – with this drug pusher called Alexandru Hajdu who lives in Thames Street. Days, he works for a Romanian theatre ticket agency off Oxford Street – which West End Central are keeping tabs on. But if we could catch Hajdu pushing, we might do a deal with him and get back to his supplier . . .'

DS Brewer had been paying close attention. 'Very good – except the Dartford man wouldn't do a deal, would he? He went down for ten. He wasn't going to cough, was he?'

Ian Webber stood silent for a moment; then he took the liberty of leaning on Brewer's desk and staring at him. 'Unless we can bring him in on another matter,' he said. 'Like suspicion of the punishment death of a Dawson boy, a Crew kid spying on him on the Barrier Estate. It's Denny Benjamin's brother Trevor who runs the Barrier Crew.'

Brewer sat back. 'You're talking about the Connor Long business?'

'Could be, sir.' Webber stood back from the desk. 'Because I've got a feeling we need to get Hajdu before one of the locals does . . .'

'Oh, yes? And whose name's in the frame for wanting to do that?'

Webber shrugged. 'Oh, some gang retaliation,' he lied.

Brewer went on staring a few seconds longer than was comfortable. Then: 'I'll give the Kent boys a push – and ask the Yard to gee-up the Marseilles police around Aix Airways.'

'Thank you, sir.'

'And good luck in court with your flasher. I'll be keen to see if the magistrates give him a month for every inch of your evidence.' The man smiled.

'They'll probably call for psychiatric reports today.'

'Could be. Or not. Best not to take guesswork too far, eh, Webber.'

'No, sir.' And Webber went back to the routine business of being a CID officer.

*

The Hajdus lived at 123 Thames Street. Mandy had kept her promise a day early and gone to the school office at the end of the afternoon, dangling her own house key at the assistant secretary and telling him that Peter Hajdu had left it on a canteen table.

'My dad's picking me up. We can run it home to him in case he can't get in.' It had been dead easy.

Amber's mobile rang. It was Sunil Dhillon, phoning again from Alexandra Palace. 'It's an early show,' he said. 'We're wrapping here at half past nine.'

'"Rama and Sita"? Shan't forget old Monkey Hanuman up there.'

'One of the Arts presenters is doing an intro to camera to show that he's there, and then a closing piece; the voice-over we're leaving to tomorrow . . .'

'Thanks for telling me, but . . .' Amber had things to do tonight; and she still had to get out of these school clothes and into something else.

'What I'm asking is, do you want to come again? I couldn't ask you yesterday, I had to clear it with Krishna . . .'

Amber looked at herself in the living room mirror. *BBC Girl!* At this rate she'd have her name stuck on the end of the programme. 'I'm gutted,' she said, 'but I promised my mum I'd dye her hair tonight.'

'Just a thought.'

'I don't like letting her down.' Meaning, letting Connor down.

'Well, perhaps some other time?'

'Be great.'

Which was a short conversation that Amber went over many times as she stood looking as if she was meeting a date, outside the entrance to the housing society flats opposite Chicky-Chick. She was depending on Hajdu not having his own transport because what she was planning was a chance meeting somewhere – but well away from his house, which would be too suspicious for a casual collision. She wasn't in the calling-a-cab league, but she had her student Oyster card for a bus.

After three quarters of an hour's waiting Hajdu took her by surprise, coming out of the Chicky-Chick side door. She'd got to the point where she was staring, but not seeing what she was staring at. The door opened, and he was already dodging cars to get to her side of the road before she realised that this bloke in a long black leather coat and flashy trainers was the man she was waiting for: the scum who could have killed her brother. And she knew him. She'd seen him somewhere before, somewhere important. He had a Nike gymsack slung across him, his face set, as he came straight for her. She took a step back, but after skipping round the last car he walked fast along the pavement to the bus stop. She followed, keeping her distance, and as she neared the bus shelter she checked the electric sign that was announcing a 472 due – going to North

Greenwich station, and when Alex Hajdu took this first bus, Amber did, too. He went upstairs, while Amber sat on the lower deck, near enough to the middle door, so she wouldn't be surprised if he suddenly got off. The next stop was East Greenwich library; but she guessed Hajdu wouldn't be off to change an Enid Blyton: he'd be going all the way, to North Greenwich and the O_2. But where had she seen him before? His face was somehow *significant*.

She always thought of the O_2 as a huge white mushroom spreading across that large arena, the small arena, the cinema, the casino, and Entertainment Avenue with its bars and cafés, a popular place with the locals as well as concert-goers – when they can afford the food and drink.

And pay for what Alex Hajdu could offer, Amber reckoned. There was no doubt the O_2 was where Hajdu was heading – where else? But Amber couldn't relax, just in case he suddenly came down those stairs and jumped off somewhere, seconds before the doors closed. So she sat tensed on the outside of her seat, left hand on the gripping bar, and right foot angled for a quick push.

But she had guessed right. He stayed upstairs on the bus until it reached the North Greenwich terminus, when he casually came down to the doors and got off – while Amber fiddled with nothing for a few seconds to be sure it was her following him, and not the other way around. She was going to keep her head down until she was ready.

She looked good, she knew that, but she hadn't overdone it, not to show up too much. She'd made up carefully, put a sparkly clip in her hair, and was suffering the April chill in a scoop-necked black vest top with a shortish skirt to match, and patent high-heeled sandals: dressed to get Hajdu willing to talk to her.

She followed him into the O_2 as he walked along Entertainment Avenue, glanced into Jimmy Monaco's, bypassed Thai Silk, obviously not his hunting ground, and sat in Feed the World with his eyes alert. All the while Amber held back, waited outside as if she was on a date, ready to let him meet whoever he was meeting. When she went for him she wanted all his attention on her.

She didn't have long to wait. Hajdu's contact soon came in, the timing good. From the look of his blue shorts and white shirt he was a boy off one of the Thames boats that turn round at the O_2. Hajdu had bought a Coca-Cola from the waitress, but this other guy didn't bother. He put something in Hajdu's hand, and Hajdu put something in his – under the table and as quick as that; and the boy went, back to his boat. Now Hajdu looked around the café. Was someone else coming to do business, or was he going to finish his drink and go? From outside Amber could see how ideal this place was for the sort of thing he did; a couple of girls serving the tables, and a man behind the counter who was too busy at his Gaggia to be noticing anything going on.

Hajdu finished his Coke. He'd either go, or someone else off one of the boats might come. Right. Amber had to act now. With a sudden adrenalin swirl inside her – *here we go* – she walked into the café and went over to his table, where he was riding a burp. She pulled out a chair and sat leaning forward, giving him a view of her cleavage. Staring at him – seeing the Hajdu family face: the pale skin, the dark eyes, the empty belly look – 'Hiya,' she said. And suddenly she knew why his face was familiar. He was the guy from Connor's funeral, who'd been staring across the aisle at PlayCo Boy.

So would he remember her?

He grunted; it was obvious he wasn't knocked out by her looks; that wasn't what he was about tonight. Now Amber wasn't too sure what she was going to do – although making a play for him definitely wasn't going to be the way in. So how about drugs . . .? Whatever she did, she had to make some impression, sound him out for a vital clue to Connor's killer – which she'd thought could well be Hajdu himself; except, the sudden thought – why would he have shown himself at the funeral?

'What you want?' he asked, his eyes fixed on her now.

'What you got?'

He said nothing. She said nothing. And Amber suddenly thought how it could be flicking through his mind that she was doing this for the police, wired up. She could be a trap. But he soon put her straight. 'You're not into nothing,' he said. 'You're the dead kid's sister. You fight with my brother.' He suddenly shot out a hand and gripped her arm, pressing it hard to the table.

'Not really a fight . . .'

He pushed his face towards her. From behind the Gaggia it could look as if he was being all lovey.

'Why did you come to Connor's funeral?' She had to know this. He shrugged. 'Beef with Barrier Crew. Show them Hajdu is not scared of them.' He gave her a thin smile. 'Always slip their ends, no problem, your brother watching corners or not.'

'And he's dead for being Barrier Crew.'

'No.' His face was suddenly serious as he looked her coldly in the face. 'Not for that.' He took his time to spell this out slowly. 'No other gang in this. Is dead for being Crew who wants out.'

What? What was that? Amber tried to get her head round what he'd just said. *Wants out?* Suicide? What did Hajdu know about Connor? A kid who mucked around and laughed like him would never want to kill himself. He was just the opposite. It was more likely this low-life here who . . . '*What?*' But she didn't push against the grip on her arm. 'Be very careful what you say to me!'

'I say the truth. Crew is nothing to me.'

Amber wanted to grab his glass with her free hand and smash it into his sneering face.

'They don' scare me. They can scare him, but they don' scare Hajdu.'

'*They* didn't frighten him. He *was* Crew. You know that. He was one of them!'

He let go of her arm. 'Not when he wants out of Crew. They don' like people want out . . .'

The shock of this sat Amber back. Did Hajdu mean what she thought he meant? 'You're saying, he wanted to get out – and they killed him?'

Hajdu didn't blink. 'I say this already, they don' like people want out. Know too much . . .'

Amber had gone cold, her arms were covered in goose bumps; but somehow her voice stayed firm. 'I've got it down it was you,' she accused. 'I've got it down he was look-out against you, dealing on the Barrier. He fingered you, and you sorted him – for the Romas.' Her eyes were needles. 'That's how I've got it.'

Hajdu shook his head. 'What's this "Romas"? There is no gang. There is me. An' Hajdu is not a killing man. No way.'

Amber sat, seeing nothing, trying to take everything in. 'So what you're telling me is –'

'Not telling you nothing. I don't know this gang. I tell

you what I hear, after. The kid want out of Crew, and Crew don' like anyone want out.' He hunched his shoulders. 'If you say this is me doing something bad like that, we find police right now, uh?' He shifted his weight and squealed back his chair, looked very serious.

But it was Amber who stood first. She got herself out of that café before Hajdu had pulled his bag from under the table to hang it across his body. That was bluff, she told herself as she ran for a bus. With what he'd got in that bag he'd no more go to the police than he'd jump off Riverview House himself. Or let himself get pushed. But bluffing over the police didn't mean he wasn't speaking the truth about Connor – that he'd fallen out with the Crew, and they'd sorted him.

And now there were others Amber urgently needed to see before planning any revenge on Alex Hajdu.

Revenge could be wild, and it could also be stupid if the wrong person got stuck.

Chapter Nineteen

After a lifetime at it Reggie Webber knew the police officer's life inside out. The end of a shift could see you going home with cuts and bruises from a violent arrest, or repetitive strain injury from hours at a keyboard. Police stomachs are not used to regular eating patterns, so a slow-cooked pot roast could be pushed aside for a baguette, or just a beer from the fridge. But whether Ian wanted something to eat or not at the end of the day, he made sure the options for both hot and cold were always there; and old as Ian was, Reggie never slept until he heard that front door shut.

And if it wasn't food for the body, he could be serving up food for thought. At around eleven that night they were in two armchairs in front of the sitting room gas fire, both drinking hot chocolate.

'Not all your urban gangs are that heavy. The news, the hype, the Home Secretary visiting Peckham in a protective vest – forget Northern Ireland in the Troubles, leave the Triads aside. Yes, you've got some serious stuff in places like north London where being caught out of your postcode can be fatal, but the murders and woundings are a pretty small proportion set against the huge membership of neighbourhood gangs around the country.' This was Reggie after five minutes of silence.

Ian Webber stared into his mug. He hadn't meant to get into talking about his job when he came through the door, but his dad liked being kept in touch, and up to now he knew everything Superintendent Brewer knew. And his father had seen all this from a very high level, so Ian listened to him, in agreement or not.

'You're seeing a gang drugs war where there could well not be one.'

'Eh?' Now Ian put down his empty mug.

'On most streets and estates they're more substitute families than postcode drugs cartels. Sure, they demand loyalty, initiations are set – but scratch 'em and most kids don't go into gangs for making money from pushing drugs, they join for what they're not getting at home ...'

'Like cold hot chocolate?'

Reggie gave his son a look. 'You already know this: these kids don't want *EastEnders* with their mums, they want laughs, friendships, being with people they actually like ... OK, perhaps with a bit of pocket money from drug pushing on the side. But the killing patches are limited, and we're well aware of them.'

'You're saying the Barrier's not likely to be part of a Noica – Dawson drug war?'

'Doesn't smell that way to me; not with trainer

laces for uniform. If it is, it's only a small scale off-shoot. No, your real grown up villains are running very different operations – illegal immigration, large-scale prostitution, country-wide drugs set-ups. What these small estate gang leaders are about is being iffy cubmasters with a bit of pushing on the streets. They're not part of any heavy narcotics scene.'

Ian let his dad have his say, although right now he just wanted his bed.

'From what I saw in Liverpool and Manchester, what these local boys do is, they buy two bob's worth off the drug importers just like any other punter, they're not in anyone's gang set-up; they pick it up on the side and sell it on around their patches for ready cash. The big stuff, for your film stars, your Members of Parliament, your captains of industry – that's all working on a different level altogether.'

Ian Webber still said nothing, he knew some of this had to make sense; and he also knew how to sit and listen.

'And these local gangs – they're not lined up like medieval armies wanting to occupy the ground standing between them. They're what they are on account of where they live, or their cultural background, or where their families come from – not from any great territorial ambition. They might knife someone because they're showing themselves on their patch – but not because the likes of your Billy Dawson or Radu Noica is some commander-in-chief who wants to take over the world.'

'You really think that?' Ian's father had been following this job very closely.

Reggie continued. 'And for what it's worth, I wouldn't mind betting your Billy Dawson doesn't even know what his driver's up to, selling to his younger brother; too dangerous – it'd lead back to him too easily if one of the kids talks.'

'Ah.'

Reggie Webber took both their empty mugs and went through to the kitchen to wash them up.

'Something to think about, anyway,' Ian said, 'although I'm not sure you're right.' But his dad didn't reply. These days when he'd had his say he went a bit deaf in one ear.

That Thursday morning there was only one place Amber was heading. To PlayCo. She'd gone to sleep with the boy from the O_2 concert on her mind, and in a dream she'd found the shop where he worked; but when she'd talked to him – in the middle of the conversation – he had morphed from being the boy at the Half Past Yesterday gig into her brother Connor, so vivid that when she woke in the middle of the night she found herself standing in his room.

'Amber? You all right?' Debra's voice had a rare clarity.

'Got up for a wee.'

'Do one for me.'

'OK.'

But Amber couldn't get Connor from her mind – and she never would, not till she'd dealt with the person who'd killed him. Not that she wanted to be rid of his memory – she just didn't want him obsessing her. So taking revenge against whoever had pushed him was always what she was going to do. And the key to finding that person could be PlayCo Boy from the O_2.

In the Yellow Pages next morning she checked the locations of the nearest PlayCo shops: she would go round them all until she'd found her man. But she hadn't even dressed when the BT phone rang.

'Amber?' It was a female: but not one of her friends.

'Yes.'

'Dawn Feldman.'

'Oh, hello . . .'

'Where are you, then? You should be here. It's an eight-thirty start today . . .'

'Eh?' *What was this?*

'Your Literature exam. It's not nine o'clock, it's eight thirty; a two hour paper . . .'

'Oh, Gawd!'

'I need a good mark off you. What state are you in?'

'Shattered.' And she was: any night with dreams of Connor left her weak and useless.

'I mean, are you up?'

'Just about.'

'Then throw a flannel round your face, clean your teeth, put something on, and get to the corner of Love Street. I'll be in my red MG.'

'What? *You?*'

'Get on with it. I'll slip you in at the back. You're not missing this one. Down to that corner, quick.'

'OK.' Caught up by Dawn Feldman's determination, Amber did as she was told and was out of the flat within eight minutes. PlayCo hadn't gone away; but then it wouldn't, would it, not in two hours?

When Webber spoke to Denny Benjamin that morning, sitting on the bonnet of his Toyota in Beckenham, it could have been his dad doing the talking. He sat there with authority, and didn't get off the car when Benjamin came towards him: instead, he folded his arms to show the street that he was police. 'Usually people come to me with information. Right now I'm coming to you.'

'I got no information.' Denny Benjamin gave the usual denial.

'You're not listening. I said, I'm coming to you with information. I'm not asking anything, I'm telling.'

'What you telling?' Denny relaxed enough to lean on a lamppost.

'Brotherly love goes deep, doesn't it, Denny?'

'Uh?'

'Young Trevor. But I'm telling you to stop supplying him. Does Billy know what you're up to? We know you phoned the Noica tip-off on Billy's behalf – we've got voice recognition – but does Billy know about your little game? Does Billy know a Barrier kid died the day a Noica man started going down for ten on the back of your phone call? Just a Barrier kid, helping to keep Trevor's little bit of pushing sweet?'

Denny Benjamin stared at Webber; there was a long pause. Eventually, 'Billy and me are like that,' Denny said, showing two fingers tight together. 'You ain't driving a wedge that way . . .'

'Oh, good. So when we pull Trevor – and then you – Billy will already know about it, will he? He'll almost be expecting it . . .'

Denny Benjamin frowned.

'What if, in court with Trevor, we put the case that the Noica tip-off was down to you, not Dawson – your attempt to help Trevor stay the main supplier on the Barrier? Billy won't be the man in the dock, but he'll be included in everything by implication, while it's you – his right hand – who dropped him in the shite . . .'

Benjamin was off that lamppost fast, fists clenched, looking as if he just might lay one on Webber. 'That's a load of crap!' he shouted. 'You ain't got a scrap o' proof.'

'That won't stop us airing it in the magistrates' court.

We won't need any legal proof – because the justice will come from Billy Dawson.'

'You're talkin' bollocks.'

'Noica's on Dawson's patch in a bigger way than the Barrier Estate, we know that. Noica was starting to hit some bigger trade this side of the river than the poor old Barrier. So where's that, Denny – the Gravesends and the Rochesters and the Maidstones, is that where he's treading on Dawson's toes? Sure as eggs it's not some run-down estate where your brother makes a fiver a week, courtesy of you.'

Benjamin stood there still looking aggressive; he said nothing.

'Anyhow, that's what we'll say it was. Just the Barrier. And the dead kid. Then won't Billy Dawson be pleased?'

Benjamin started pacing. 'What you want?' he demanded.

'Nothing. I told you, I'm telling, not asking.' Now Ian Webber slowly pushed himself off Benjamin's bonnet and dusted his hands. 'So you keep an eye on your postman, and make sure you don't miss that court summons.' And he walked on past his parked Vauxhall as if it had nothing whatever to do with Thames Reach CID.

If Denny Benjamin was a fixer – a driver, a right hand man, a salesman, a bodyguard – his younger brother Trevor was a leader. Denny had left the family home young because Trevor was already having all the say-so; and when Trevor said he wanted something – like a bedroom to himself – he got it, even with a strong Jamaican mother. No one would think of the boys as brothers – not remarkable given they had different fathers – Denzel tall and dark skinned with short, thick hair and good bone structure. Trevor paler – his father was white – with a biggish head, a fleshy nose and mouth, and long straightened auburn hair, his eyes a milky brown that boiled easily. He, too, was tall from their mother, and wore long, collarless shirts that hung loose outside his trousers: always a good cover for 'carrying'.

The two brothers were sharing a shopping trolley in Tesco's in Lewisham, talking together where no one was going to give them a second look.

'This filth – what the hell does he know? I mean, like, *know*?' Trevor Benjamin chose oven chips and threw them into the trolley Denny was wheeling.

'Too bloody much, that's what he knows . . .'

'OK, I'll lay it out another way. Don' you reckon he's flyin' a kite? What can the bastard prove?' Trevor threw in another bag of oven chips.

Denny stopped the trolley. 'Listen to what I'm saying – he's not goin' there. If he's flyin' a kite 'e's gonna fly it at the magistrates, so he c'n tell Billy what we're doin".

Trevor pulled the trolley on from the front, to the

ice cream. 'So why not go route one to Dawson, if that's his pitch? Why ponce about wiv magistrates if he can go direct?' Walls Cornish Vanilla. 'No – he was gettin' you goin', you dill, he was runnin' it at you to see what you done.' He looked around the store. 'An' you played his game, din't you, made him right? Right now, prob'ly, he's tailed you gettin' to me – an' here we both are, talkin' turkey. You sucka! Shopping on a Thursday morning! Now he knows what track to take.'

Denny walked on, looking all around, checking the next aisle, and the next. He came back. 'Can't see him.'

Trevor snorted a laugh. "Course you can't. He's prob'ly dressed up as that ol' lady in the 'lectric cart.'

'It's bloody serious!' Denny rounded on his brother. 'He's got me marked for causin' Noica's lot to push a kid off a balcony . . .'

Trevor leaned over the trolley and pushed it on. 'Oh, the kid.'

'Yeah, the kid. They know he was Crew, which comes back to you, clever Trevor. So it ain't jus' my problem wi' Billy we're talkin' about. You throwed a few dollars at the mother to put her off thinkin' it could be you – I drove you there: big favour.'

Trevor stopped and stood up tall. 'Yeah.' His flippant mood suddenly changed. 'I smashed the phone an' ate the sim card – but there's a sister with a bloody sharp eye.'

'Well, then.'

'The ol' woman's a piss-artist, no one's gonna believe a word she ever says – but I'm not happy about the girl . . .' Trevor started piling the trolley with packet after packet of petit pois, emptied the entire freezer section of peas. 'So we'll jus' have to both watch our backs, won' we?' And he walked briskly from the store, leaving Denny and the trolley where they were in the middle of an aisle.

Amber came out of the drama room, picking her way carefully between the small examination tables; which were the same as she felt – collapsible. Two hours before, she'd made it to the corner of Love Street, sat knees up under her chin in Mrs Feldman's small car, been hurried through the school and ushered in at the back of the drama room, where heads were already bent over the first question. She didn't know what she'd put down on those sheets of paper. The questions had been kind but not easy, and she'd written what was probably a load of rubbish till they'd been told to lay down their pens. Now she was on another agenda – the really important task that was driving her.

First, though, she went to find Mrs Feldman in her office: she owed her a word. How many deputy heads would come to get you to take an exam? She didn't want to push it with the woman, but the light shining from under the door seemed to say 'wait' not 'come back later', so she sat on a comfortable chair; she'd give it a few minutes – then there was urgent stuff to do.

She didn't have to wait long. After a few minutes later a Sikh father came out of the office and left – and the deputy head's eyes lit up as she saw Amber.

'How did it go? How were the questions?'

Amber stood, shrugging. 'Don't know. The questions were OK, it was the answers I had trouble with . . .'

Dawn Feldman laughed. 'I wanted you there, Amber.' She fixed her eyes on her. 'I'm on your case: you're not selling snacks at Charlton Athletic all your life.'

'Anyhow, I came to say thank you.'

'Glad to do it. Now what – school dinner? Or would that be breakfast to you?'

'Not really hungry.' But Amber knew she had something else to say to Mrs Feldman before she went. It was important, given what she'd done for her that morning. 'Just want to say – I'm sorry if I let you down in that exam. I have stuff going on.'

'I know you do.' The woman took Amber's arm and steered her into the office. 'Your brother died, and you're not going to accept that he fell.'

'That's right . . .'

'So, where are you with that? Was what happened in the girls' lavatories connected in some way?'

Amber blew out her cheeks. Dawn Feldman knew everything. 'Sort of.'

She sat them down on her sofa. 'So what's your theory? Where are you going with it?'

235

Eh? Was Amber hearing this? And should she answer? How incriminating would that be when she finally did what she had to do?

'You think Connor was pushed.'

Amber nodded.

'By a rival gang?'

'Could be.'

'*Could* be? Who else would do it, then?'

Amber sat silent, pressing both hands between her knees as if they might fly up and say secret stuff in sign language.

'He *was* in a gang?'

Amber nodded. 'But he wanted out . . .' Oh, God, she'd said too much already.

'Was it his own gang, then? Would his own gang do it? Community police tell me getting out is one of the hardest things in the world.' Mrs Feldman's voice was soft and sincere. She talked real life the way she talked education. 'Well, I'll tell you who killed him.'

Amber's head shot up.

'We killed him. Society. School. The way things are.' She stopped. 'Do you want me to go on, because I'll stop . . .'

Amber looked into the teacher's eyes. 'No, go on.'

'First, your parents. They failed him. A violent father . . . maybe not to him, but violent, fetches up in prison; a mother who goes walkabout all the time, lives her life outside her family . . .'

'But a loving sister.' Already Amber was crying. 'He had a really loving sister. I loved that boy to bits!'

'But you couldn't do it all, not on your own, could you?' The teacher had her arm round Amber's shoulder. 'And the schools he should've gone to have got to pick up their share of the blame. We ought to give kids some of the sense of belonging they find in the gangs.'

And that was down to the lousy primary headteacher who hadn't given Connor a chance: who was nothing like the heads whose kids made huge puppets and danced and battled in the Ramayana. *Keying his car was the least Amber should have done to that scum.*

'True caring and tough love, that's what Connor needed – and apart from you he didn't get it.'

Amber couldn't see the carpet pattern through her wet eyes. 'Not you, Dawn,' she said, 'don't include you.' And she put her arms around the woman and cried into her suit, not believing what she'd just called her. But neither, as she left that special room, did she regret it for one moment.

Chapter Twenty

There are four PlayCo shops in the Yellow Pages: one in Eltham, one in Lewisham, one in Woolwich, one in Surrey Quays – but none in Thames Reach. The rest of the chain weren't shown in Amber's edition, but she had a gut feeling anyway that the O_2 boy would work fairly near to home. Well, she'd see.

She went to Woolwich first. Wearing her old three-quarter-length mac, she looked in through the windows of the shop, beyond the posters. There was a small queue at the counter, two people serving; and without going inside Amber could see that neither of them was her boy: one was a fat girl in a blue PlayCo T-shirt, the other some sort of male manager in a suit. OK, Amber's target could be on a tea break – but she could hardly go in and ask, could she? So she headed for the 54 bus stop for Lewisham. Right now she could do with Sunil on his scooter, taking a day off; but at last the bus came, and half an hour later she was in Lewisham High Street, looking vainly for PlayCo – which turned out to have gone, closed down, with a small bank branch sitting new and empty of customers instead. The games shop could just have moved locations, though, perhaps into the shopping precinct, because games were still big, weren't they? So Amber asked in the bank, went up to a young woman sitting at a cleared desk with a laptop, who straight off shook her head.

'They wouldn't pay the rent when it wen' up,' she told Amber. 'They'll show theirselves somewhere soon.'

'There's not a PlayCo in Lewisham at all?'

'Not as we speak. Not as far as I've been told.' The girl half turned away. 'Can I help you with anythink else?'

'No thanks.'

Which left Amber looking for the bus to take her to Eltham – and at last her persistence paid off – because looking in through the PlayCo window in Eltham High Street – yes! – there was her man behind the counter, one of three people in blue. It was definitely him, she'd know that gel-spiked hair and the ear stud anywhere.

She was second in the queue; but when the wrong assistant became free she let someone slide in front of her so she could get to the one she wanted.

'Come down . . .'

She was quickly in front of him; and if he recognised her from the other night at the O_2 he didn't give it away.

'Fill me out a form for a reward card,' she told him.

'A reward card?'

'Yeah.' She took one from a display at his side and pushed it in front of him. 'Reward card. Put down my name, address, all that . . .'

'No, you take these away and bring them back.'

'*You* fill it in. I'm illiterate – can't spell "Barrier", let alone "Crew".'

Now he stared at her.

'Filling that in keeps us talking – and if you don't do what I say I'll shout and scream and tell all the High Street you just called me a white whore.'

The black guy kept his cool; his expression didn't alter – but as Amber looked ready to do what she'd threatened, he called across the shop to a colleague. 'Colin, c'n you take over here – I'm filling in an agreement . . . ?'

'No prob, Jacko.'

So that was his name.

Colin came over – no fuss – and Jacko picked up a clipboard, 'Come wi' me, please,' taking Amber into a corner of the shop away from the windows. 'What do you want – coming in here?' he hissed at her.

"Cos I've got just one question to ask – then I'm gone.' She looked around. 'It's Perkins,' she said loudly, 'Deborah – with an "h".' Jacko actually wrote 'Deborah Perkins' on the form. 'That's it, just look as if you're writing. You know me, don't you? From the O_2, Half Past Yesterday.'

'Yeah, I know you. Listen, sis, I helped you all I could. I played you straight, I told you trust stuff . . .'

'Hundred and thirty-eight Coxwell Road', Amber said, pointing to the form. 'Cox as in apple, not as in trousers . . .' She pushed the clipboard down. 'He wanted out, didn't he – Connor? My brother wanted out: why didn't you tell me that?'

'Could it be 'cos I didn't know . . .?'

'No, it couldn't be. You knew.' Amber twisted her head around. 'Are you ready for this?' She took in a deep, loud, breath, as if she really was about to scream the place down.

'Yeah, I knew.'

'Why, then? Why did he want out? He didn't act any different at home.'

'Don' really know – think it was something to do with the corners thing.'

'The looking out for Romas?'

'Not just them, the other stuff – watchin' our cars, the flats, any taggers from Charlton slippin'. He had to climb to the one place, best view.' Jacko showed clean palms. 'Then he tol' someone he wanted to climb where *he* wanted to climb . . .'

'So –' She turned herself towards Jacko, into him, almost nose to nose, tense again. 'So what usually happens when someone wants out of the Crew? What happens to them?'

Jacko shook his head. 'Dunno. Never tried it. Wouldn't, mate.'

With a loud crack she whacked the clipboard from

beneath, hit it up almost into his face. 'SE18 9TE – seventh floor.' And she didn't drop her customer voice to add, 'It's a hell of a long way up – looking down!'

Jacko had written just 'SE18' before Amber pinched her thumb and finger round his diamond stud and pulled his ear close to her mouth. 'Did you do anything, Jackson?' she wanted to know.

He carefully reclaimed his ear. 'No, I never. You can shout an' dance an' kick up a fuss, but I swear I don' know what happened.'

Colin was walking over. 'Everything all right over here?'

'Pukka. No prob.' Jacko folded the form and put it in an envelope. 'Cheers, then, Deborah – we'll be in touch . . .'

'We'll see, Jacko,' Amber grated. 'We'll see.'

And she had never sounded quite so much like a Debra in all her life.

That night on the Barrier Estate Jacko found Trevor Benjamin in the basement laundry room of Jimmy Seed house, waiting in his long, floral shirt to meet a regular crack customer.

'Yeah?'

There was an old man doing his weekly wash. Benjamin pulled Jacko round behind the machines, bent with him as if they were inspecting a leak.

'What?'

'Connor – the kid . . .'

'What about him? He's dead.' But Trevor Benjamin's eyes were a lot less 'don't-care' than his voice.

'His sister . . .'

'Yeah?'

'Come in my shop. She knows he wanted out. But I never told her that, Trev.'

'You better not 'ave. Where'd she get it from, then? I give her ol' lady some money – lookin' all tight an' fam'ly.'

'Dunno. Got it from somewhere; but prob'ly not Crew. Only the thing is . . .'

'The thing is *what*, Beckford? What's her beef?'

Jackson Beckford put his head round the machine, where the old man was watching his drum churning. 'She's gonna get someone, I know she is. She's a right fiery cat. An' she's not gonna go away.'

'Oh, no?' Trevor Benjamin walked away from him, back to stand leaning against the wall again, waiting for his customer. 'We'll 'ave to see about that, won' we?'

Which was Jacko dismissed, but his warning delivered like loyal Crew.

It was only confirmation Amber wanted. While the gang itself would never say, the name she'd heard on the estate for its leader was Trevor Benjamin. And Amber knew that for Connor to be pushed, the order had to have come from the gang leader. Never mind society doing it, that meant Trevor Benjamin was the real murderer. Before she took her revenge, though, she had to be cast-iron sure.

Which was where Sunil Dhillon came in. He could find out. He had his contacts – including the police, who seemed to trust him. After all, nothing had been on television about all this, had it? So Amber rang Sunil. She'd had to turn down his invitation to go again to the *Ramayana* – and she regretted that: not only not seeing the show again, but being with him; somehow she felt very comfortable when he was around. This commitment was on a different level, though.

'Amber! How's it going?' Immediately his voice was warm and welcoming.

'It's OK.'

'How are *you*?'

'I'm good. Did an exam this morning. Did crap, of course!'

He laughed. 'Wait and see. Don't put yourself down.'

There was a long pause.

'I'm sorry I couldn't make it to Alexandra Palace. How did it go?'

'The Arts presenter made a cock-up of his piece and had to re-do it in the studio; stupid, because that made nonsense of him being there. Other than that, it was fine. Wait till it goes out in June.'

Another awkward pause.

'Sunil – could you check someone out for me? I've got a name for what happened to Connor.' Now she had to lie. 'Before I go to the police, I want to be sure I've got the right one.'

'You're going to the police? You're not—' His voice didn't sound any different – but did Sunil believe her? 'You've changed your mind about what you want to do?'

'You were right. It's best.'

'What's the name you want checking?'

'Benjamin. Trevor Benjamin.'

'Trevor Benjamin. In what connection?'

'Just tell me what anyone's got on him. I'll know then.'

Sunil laughed, but it wasn't humour. 'Being a bit cagey, aren't you?'

'You bet I am.'

'All right, then. I'll get back to you.'

'Tonight?'

'You can go to them any time. The police *do* work Fridays and weekends, you know.'

'Just to be sure,' Amber said.

And half an hour later, Sunil phoned back. But he was the cagey one this time. 'I'll do a deal,' he said. 'Before I tell you what I've found out, you've got to make me a promise . . .'

Anything. Amber was playing her own game so much in this that she'd say anything to be sure that name was the right one: nothing else in life mattered a toss compared with settling this debt for Connor. He wasn't the sort to ever rest in peace, but his spirit would be free to dazzle the angels.

'Are you there?'

'Yes,' Amber said, 'I'm here.'

'You're promising me something, then?'

'I'm promising.'

'Thank you. Will you come with me to the Television News Awards on Sunday night? It's at BAFTA, in Piccadilly. We're not up for one and Krishna Roy can't go, so she's given me her invitation.'

'Sounds good,' Amber said. Although where she would be on Sunday night was anybody's guess – celebrating, or on the run, or denying everything at a police station . . .

'You're on. So what's the answer? On Trevor Benjamin?'

'Well, according to my source Trevor Benjamin runs the gang on your estate, the Barrier Crew. Is that what you've got?'

'Fits,' said Amber. Her inside went electric – with the dread thrill of knowing now for certain who she was going to kill.

'His brother's called Denzel; works at the Midnight Express night club in Deptford; but don't involve his name; my source was very sensitive about that.'

'Whatever you say.'

'Apparently, Trevor Benjamin gets in Midnight

Express himself.'

Then she'd have seen him there, Amber thought.

'Who are you going to? Police-wise?'

Her reply came fast. 'I'm going local,' she said, ignoring his question; because she *was* going local – just as far as this Trevor Benjamin.

'I'll pick you up around seven, then, on Sunday.'

You might or you might not: that didn't come into it any more.

'You there? Sunday. I'll pick you up around—'

'Yeah, seven. Cheers. See you, Sunil.'

'See you.'

But would he have realised that she hadn't bothered to ask him what she should wear to go to BAFTA? Was she so focused on what she was going to do that she was slipping up on small details?

Chapter Twenty-one

Amber did her best to avoid Dawn Feldman at Thames Reach Academy. She still didn't regret the way she'd spoken to the deputy head the day before – treating her almost like a sister – but she wanted to leave it at that. Saying sorry and colouring up like a fool was what she didn't want, so Amber's journey through the timetabled day wasn't going to take her anywhere near the offices.

And then at lunchtime there the woman was, coming out from the canteen, with two boys and a football.

'Amber Long!' Mrs Feldman sent the boys to go and wait outside her office. 'I felt really proud, reading your Literature Mock answers.' She was looking at Amber. 'Some thoughtful takes, Mr Pewtrell's shown us a thing or two with your form's work . . .'

'Yeah . . .'

'But I got the feeling it was your own idea in the "Dream" answer to draw parallels between Puck with Oberon and Hanuman with Rama, both loyal and magical servants making things happen? None of the others thought of that.'

'It just struck me,' Amber said.

Lauren and Oki came up; and Amber didn't want any more of this. Being singled out helps you lose your friends pronto.

'Well done all of you. I'm proud.'

'An' I'm glad it's over!' Oki said.

'Do we do the *Ramayana* here at Thames Reach these days?' Mrs Feldman questioned the three.

All shook their heads.

'So where did Hanuman come from?' she quizzed Amber. God, the woman wasn't going to go away.

'I saw it being acted.'

'Ah. Well, great stuff. Original thinking,' she said as she went to sort the football boys. 'Great stuff, all three.' But that sounded almost like an afterthought.

'But she din't say how I got ol' Oberon down for a kinky weirdo!' Oki complained. 'The guy who wants his little Indian boy.'

'Did you put that?' Amber asked.

"Course she didn't.' Lauren was walking on into the lunch room. 'Leave out the geniuses, the rest of us have to play their answers game.'

Oki followed her. And for the first time since the family tragedy, Amber felt their cool as the canteen door swung between them.

'Oi. Hold on.'

They stopped, but slowly.

'I'm not any genius – so don't come it. My Connor

was like Puck, and he was also like Hanuman; it was Connor did it, just being Connor.' She shrugged apologetically. 'If what I wrote was any good.'

'Oh, it sounded good to me,' said Lauren; and then jealousy seemed to evaporate. 'But being a genius won't stop you being my mate,' she said. 'So now I'm going to buy us both a burger.'

Which she did, but when Amber ate it, it seemed to have no taste at all.

First, Amber chose what she would wear – which ended up being the outfit she'd worn trying to snare Alexandru Hajdu. Making herself up, she deliberately over-did the eyes and lips; and she sprayed herself to a coughing fit with Debra's 'show-me-to-the-bedroom' scent. So far, so lawful. And then she went to the kitchen drawer for the black-handled vegetable knife she was going to use on Trevor Benjamin, the one that fitted just right into her leather shoulder bag.

Jostling with Debra as they both got ready to go out, Amber was geeing herself up all the time. Knifing was a deadly business, doing it would change her life completely – and in the middle of dusting shimmery powder on her shoulders she had to go into Connor's bedroom to fire up the flames that were cooling as the time drew nearer. But where she thought she'd stand and cry at his pathetic mended bed; at opening his wardrobe and putting her head in amongst his clothes;

at pulling out that favourite seaside picture of him –
her eyes were bone dry, and her stomach wouldn't
churn with the old outrage. Now that she was almost
ready to go out her courage was failing, and she was
running out of confidence. Not intention: she was
definitely going to do it: but now that she was
this close, the drive to stick someone in revenge was
fading fast.

Which had to be natural, she told herself. Nerves.
Just wait till she saw his hateful face. Anger would
do it then. Sheer anger.

She'd got it planned. From what Sunil had told her
she knew where she'd go to find him; where she and
her friends and half the Thames Reach Friday-nighters
went these days – to the Midnight Express nightclub
along at Deptford. If he was the one she thought he
was, she'd definitely seen him there when she was with
the others, just never taken much notice of him. And
now he was in her focus, was he the same guy who'd
given cash to Debra at the Captain Cook? She'd soon
know. And tonight she was going alone. Tonight she
wasn't going to involve Lauren, or Mandy or Narinder
Oki; and if they happened to be there, she'd do her best
to give them a miss. Because this wasn't their vendetta:
it was Long versus Benjamin, exclusive.

She decided she'd get in once the place was jumping.
She and the others usually went early because of family
curfews on Narinder and Oki; also there was no

queuing outside the club at nine, while there was at ten, and worse at eleven. But tonight she would suffer the queuing; the later the better, really, to get in with a knife and stick Trevor Benjamin. Bag searches at busy times are a very token business.

All of which meant Amber had to hang around in the flat once Debra had gone off somewhere. And the place was spooky, her all made-up and ready to go, sitting on the settee watching rubbish telly but seeing nothing. The hairspray and the talcum had settled well into the carpets, and her resolve was drifting down there with them.

The television set went suddenly blank in a botched change-over between programmes – and for an instant Amber saw her reflection on the screen, sitting there not being too careful with her legs. God, she looked a sight, like something out of a dodgy movie. But it was a look that might get her close to Trevor Benjamin

So she went then. Early or late, if she was going to do what she was going to do, she was going to have to do it now or she never would.

It was about half past nine when she joined a short queue of girls outside the entrance of the club, and then had no bother at all getting in. Her 'pass' was the tenner in her hand from Debra's purse, and she was waved through by a tall, tough, white guy who hardly gave her a second look as he fixed her plastic wristband: his language a grunt and a cocking of his head in the direction of the pay box. And Amber was inside Midnight Express – shoulder bag, knife and all – hidden in the lining till she was through the door.

The place had its own smell. The old cinema had left its years of smoking stained into the layers of paint on the walls, which, mixed with roll-on and sweat gave off a forbidden sort of musk. But to Amber that Friday night Midnight Express smelt only of danger. Her eyes darted all around the place, looking, looking, looking for Trevor Benjamin.

And she nearly said something out loud when she spotted him; yes – she was sure it was who she thought it was, the one who'd made a show of pretend sympathy to her mother – which she knew now had been intended to take the Crew out of the frame for Connor's death; that pimply skin, the fat nose, and the long hair. Her hands went sticky, she had to wipe them down her skirt, and her neck went stiff. Over there was Connor's murderer. For the first time since knowing what he'd done, she reckoned she was staring at the man she was going to kill.

Except – how would she get at him? Because, what was he doing right now? He was dodging in and out behind the bar, taking a drink to the DJ up on the rostrum, and then a tray-full to a table of girls and a man in a suit who were sitting near to her. She wanted to get away with this revenge, not get caught for it, planned to be in a tight pack where people hardly notice someone who's slipped to the floor; and by the time anyone does, there's the chance to be well on the way out. But she couldn't get at him while he was in the eye like this.

But what was that he said – and they said – when he brought a group their drinks?

'How's Marseilles today?'

'Sunny, Trev, sunny . . .'

Trev! Trevor Bloody Benjamin. She was right. Double certain. So she'd get off to a corner, and wait for her chance. He'd probably dance later – even the DJ came down sometime during the evening. But she felt weird waiting, leaning against the wall on her own. She never came clubbing without friends, nor did most people – not unless they were pushers or pimps – and they rarely stood around and waited, they worked the floor. While what was worse, the music wasn't anything you could get up and dance to on your own. The regular DJ, Fat Leonard – so skilled at whipping everyone into a froth with a string of hits – was playing the ballad of the year, 'No Way to Go', the Half Past Yesterday number, and there was no way Amber could get up on that floor without one of her mates.

Which was when she was suddenly hit by jaw-dropping fright. Up to now what she was going to do had been a plan. Soon it would be an act – the act of murder: the real, final thing. And the thought of this nearly being the moment brought her out in a sweat.

'Yeah, hot, i'n it?' A tall black guy with a serious face was standing next to her. 'Don' I know you? Seen you goin' in the Captain Cook that day?' This man had crept up on her, coming along the wall from nowhere.

'Did you?'

'Don' forget a beautiful face, me.'

'Funny, I always remember an ugly mug, but I don't know you.' Amber had come off the wall, the lights playing around the nightclub changing their faces.

'You know my bro . . .'

And now Amber knew who this man was. It was Trevor Benjamin's brother. Connor's killer's brother!

"E wants a word. Had a lot o' time for your kid.'

'Yeah?' What did Trevor Benjamin want with her? It was what she wanted with him that counted.

'Look, 'e's comin' over . . .'

And he was. Pushing in a direct line through the pairs of girls came Amber's target. Now would be it – if only his rotten brother wasn't around. And anyway, where she was against the wall there was no way she could get a hand to that knife.

The Benjamin she wanted was standing in front of her now, eyeing her, and it was all she could do not to spit in his hateful face. His brother still stood at her side, definitely ruling out any chance of her getting at that knife.

'So you're Trevor,' she said, staring back at him. 'The big man.' He didn't blink. 'Are you a big man, Trevor?'

His brother shifted on the wall.

'On occasion,' Trevor said. 'When there's need . . .'

'Good.' Amber didn't know where this was coming from, this improvisation. Probably because right now knifing was on hold, and some other set-up might be needed. Getting Trevor Benjamin in a surprise attack while he looked down her top wasn't going to happen right here, not now she'd been spotted for who she was.

'You knew my little brother . . .'

'I knew your little bruvver.' Trevor Benjamin hadn't moved a muscle, hadn't changed his stance, nor did he as the music played another ballad. 'Good little younger 'e was.'

Amber nodded. 'He would've been. He was a terrific kid.'

Where was this going? What was in Benjamin's mind?

'What you come here for?' Trevor asked.

'I come here a lot. Waiting for my mates.'

'Yeah?' He looked around.

'*And* I wanted to see you,' Amber had suddenly got a line to take, him talking about Crew brethren.

'That's handy.'

She looked at the floor; aware of those body language give-aways that she mustn't show while she lied her head off; because she had to get this killer on his own, with his guard down. 'I want to be what he was,' she said; and she laughed modestly: 'Not as

256

a climber and a corners girl,' she said; 'more like a . . .'

'A *what*, Am-ba?'

He still hadn't moved a muscle. Was she trying hard enough? 'Do you have, like . . .' She deliberately allowed a long, long pause; took a breath, and, doing it, straightened her top with one hand, lowering its wide neckline to show a sparkly shoulder. 'Do you go in for Crew *partners* – that kind of thing?'

Now Trevor shifted, a bit.

'You gave my mum some dosh . . .'

"S'right, I did. Crew for Crew.'

'But it's not dosh I need. I need Crew itself. He died as Crew, and whatever he wanted at the end – because Connor always went his own way – if the Romas killed him, I want in against anyone who isn't Barrier.' She had to keep up this part of the pretence. 'On my own level . . .'

'Well, now.' Trevor Benjamin gave her something like a smile. 'I said you bein' here was handy, because we're talking the same language, sister.'

Amber tried to look quietly, publicly happy. 'There's got to be some sort of initiation, hasn't there?' she asked: lips and eyes.

The other Benjamin snorted. Trevor Benjamin went serious. 'Oh, there will be one of them,' he said. 'So 'ow about roun' my flat, Sunday night – 'bout seven. On your level, like you say.'

'Where's that?' Amber asked – as unfazed as she

could muster. 'Your flat?'

'Jimmy Seed House. 901. Ninth floor, next to the lift.'

In his flat? She'd planned to do it here, in a crowd, getting away from the scene before he hit the floor. Then she'd improvised – but, on her own in his flat? She'd have to be clever – and she'd have to be brave. 'You got it, Big Man,' she heard herself saying. 'After. After we've got to know each other a bit. On our own.' She was thinking hard. She wanted what this place offered, but it couldn't be here any more with Benjamin's brother about. So where, where was like this? She was desperate for an idea to come. 'The Tramshed,' she suddenly said. 'Sunday night.' The jazz floor there heaved like this – would give her as good a chance to knife him as Midnight Express. 'A bit of jazz to relax us, then back to your place . . .'

'O-K. Then I'll give you a real Crew gettin'-in.' He smiled a horrible smile.

'I'm relying on that. Can't wait. Oh, I'll see you outside Jimmy Seed. Seven. We'll go down the Tramshed together.'

'You got it.'

With a quick look at each other the brothers went – neither saying a word as they crossed the floor back to the bar; while Fat Leonard gave them time to get clear before he started on a playlist of hit music.

Which Amber missed; because she was already heading for the exit: mission failed, but a chance lined up, if she'd got the skill and the guts to do it. So to buoy herself up going home on the bus, she told herself that she was just like Sita, knowing what was going to happen to the ten-headed demon, Ravena – and knowing now the new location in the jungle where that would be.

Detective Superintendent Brewer was in the CID office that Saturday morning, wearing the weekend dress code of sweater and open-necked shirt, prior to a 'meet' at a sporting venue.

And Mr Brewer was in a cheerful Saturday mood when he called Ian Webber into his office. 'Got a minute, Ian? So, where are we with Dawson and his operation? You got anywhere with Benjamin an' his shenanigans?'

Webber stood to attention before the DS's desk, also Saturday morning style in his suede shoes. 'I think I might have done something on the local level, sir,' he said. 'Regarding our patch . . .'

'Tell me.'

'Dawson's probably not that big round here, not with his main dealings. It's small-fry locally, that's my view,' Webber said. 'What's going onto the estates is something on the side, peripheral, I think I've established that . . .'

'How come?' Brewer was fiddling with the tight top of a bottle of Tipp-ex.

'I played a bluff with Denny Benjamin – and his reaction told me I'm heading in the right direction . . .'

'Which is where?' The top came off the Tipp-ex, and Brewer was back, quizzing a look at Webber.

'My thinking is, if Dawson was threatened by a big player like Noica, he's got to have a biggish operation of his own. If all Dawson was importing were the bits and pieces we see locally, he'd never have had cause to set Revenue and Customs onto Noica's Dartford operation . . .'

'That makes sense . . .'

'So he's bigger than just this quarter of south London. I think we should be liaising with divisions further uptown and where the bigger money is, in Kent and Surrey – take a look at what they've got going on. Thames Reach is kids' stuff to Dawson . . .'

Brewer sniffed. 'We'll take a look at that in due course.' So he wasn't committing himself right now. 'And your local Romanian – what's his name?'

'Hajdu. Alexandru Hajdu.'

'Where does he fit in?'

Webber stretched, standing there. 'I think he's small time; selling-on the stuff Noica lets him have for his own use.' He stopped, a sudden thought. 'For all I know that's how he gets paid for being a sandwich-board man . . .'

DS Brewer sat back. 'Right, meanwhile have a look at this. A message from Marseilles.' He lifted his elbow from what was beneath it, and handed Webber a file with a sheet of paper clipped to its front.

It was a thinnish collection of papers in a manilla folder marked up as ILLEGAL SUBSTANCES – DIVISIONAL.

The top paper was typed in French capitals, but it carried a translation beneath, its message a welcome sight to Webber.

THE ANGLO-FRENCH AVIATION COMPANY, AIX AIRWAYS, HAS BEEN SUSPENDED FROM OPERATING THE COMMERCIAL ROUTE BETWEEN MARSEILLES AIRPORT AND LONDON BIGGIN HILL, EFFECTIVE IMMEDIATELY.

IRREGULARITIES WITH CARGO HAVE BEEN DISCOVERED WHICH ARE THE SUBJECT OF SCRUTINY BY BORDER CUSTOMS OFFICERS.

And, in English, in ink: '*On the evidence already passed by the French, as a precautionary step the British Aviation Authority is not contesting this decision on behalf of Aix Airways.*'

The French paragraph was signed by someone in French Customs; while the English was signed by a Commander in Revenue and Customs at Scotland Yard.

'That's very good, sir.'

'Could be.' Brewer was getting up, ready to go, using the Tipp-ex on a small coffee stain on his cuff. Now would be the moment, after this small success brought about by Ian Webber's Biggin Hill tail, to offer to take him to the police club for a pint. But, 'Good work,' Webber's superior said, 'so far.'

And the DC was left to console himself that if Billy Dawson's Marseilles supply line had been cut off as Radu Noica's had been previously, then at least the Thames Reach patch was going to be a bit better off.

Chapter Twenty-two

That Sunday the Benjamin brothers were quite clear between themselves what they were going to do – and everything was ready to do it. The LSD pills were in Trevor's pocket, the syringe, needle, and heroin solution were handy in his kitchen, and the Midnight Express van was parked outside Denny's Beckenham address; while the tidal River Thames would be running out early evening, into the Estuary and the North Sea. Amber Long would be a junkie from a broken family, her body filled with 'H' and her dirty needle and a packet of condoms in her pocket; a sad case just like her suicidal brother. Which would be her out of the way, and a great hole in the kite Webber had been flying.

Amber was ready, too. Saturday had been hell, because everything was supposed to have been over on Friday night, and it wasn't. Since then she hadn't been able to settle to anything. Lauren had phoned on Saturday morning and invited her over to see a concert on HD, but Amber had said she couldn't go out, she and Debra were clearing Connor's cupboards; so she'd see

Lauren on Monday. If she didn't get caught – and she was determined that she wouldn't. She'd knife Trevor Benjamin and slip out of the Tramshed before his body hit the floor. Well, she could only hope.

Like that, Amber had dragged her life limply through Saturday, with a fizzing in her gut that wouldn't go away; and then Sunday had to be endured, every long minute of it until seven o'clock. She rehearsed her moves again. Standing in her bedroom she put her right hand to her side and by feel alone she slipped the tongue of her shoulder bag from its slot and lifted the flap – but sometimes she fumbled pulling out the knife. She went through it again, got the knife out all right this time, but she preferred the handle with the grip this way, not that. Once more, she went through it – and on this slick move, she gripped the handle hard, pulled out the knife, and stabbed the blade into her pillow. Dead. But not a triumph: it just had to be done. Didn't it? A couple of weeks ago killing her brother's murderer had definitely seemed the right thing to do, no question; and on Friday night she'd gone to Midnight Express to do it. But after forty-eight hours the thought of what she was intending hung low over her. Amber Long, student, poor family background – but with a brain some people thought was worth developing – was intending to kill a man. As far as Trevor Benjamin was concerned Amber Long was going to be God. This wasn't going to be a beating like her father would have dished out; this was worse, the ultimate. Killing. It was a huge thing she was going to do, outside all common experience; something that would change her own life for ever – even if she got away with it.

With the enormity of it all she suddenly sat down on her bed. *What? What* was she going to do – Amber Long who indoors and out lived in a London minefield, who had so far trodden through it without blowing herself up like Debra, and her dad, and Connor? A girl who got pats on the back from Dawn Feldman for surviving – *what* was she planning to do? Murder. And why was she going to do it? Was it out of guilt for being that survivor, and for not helping Connor more, was that the real reason? Could it be this knifing was for her own conscience, and not for revenge at all – the only way she could hold her head up high? She stood up as suddenly as she'd sat. Leave those thoughts, they were too uncomfortable. All she wanted now was to stop having to think about it and get on and do it, get rid of this stomach-twisting agony. She walked from room to room, couldn't settle anywhere or to anything. The walls of the flat – those same stupid patterns – they all seemed to be moving in on her; she felt so tense and imprisoned she wanted to scream, and bang on the kitchen door with a tin mug. Anything to get out and get going. Was this what her father's life was like, banged-up in Strangeways?

At last, at long, hellish last, when the kitchen clock said six twenty-five she got dressed: she took a tenner from her mother's jar, left an IOU: and then what a relief to get out at last and go to do what she'd been planning. She shouted something to Debra who was groaning in her bedroom. Again, she checked her shoulder bag for the knife, the right way round, and she walked fast out of the flat without looking back – nothing and no one on her mind now except Trevor Vermin Benjamin.

The Barrier Estate was empty of people early on that Sunday evening. Locked cars filled all the parking spaces; a television played through an open window on the spring night; a curtain blew out from a second floor flat, riding on reggae. Amber walked through between the tower blocks, from Bartram House, past Riverview where Connor had been thrown off, and carefully stepped around where his chalked outline could still be seen, faint on the concrete. She edged herself past the wilted flowers leaning against the nearest wall: on her way to pay her own tribute in her own just fashion: along to the block nearest to the river, Jimmy Seed House. This was where Trevor Benjamin lived. This was where she was going to meet him, to go with him to the Tramshed. And only one of them would come back.

At the entry to the block she had to detour around a badly parked white van to get to the entrance lobby with its keypad and squawk-box. And now this was the moment. She'd phone up and tell him she was here. She stood and faced the intercom, final thoughts. She could press that first buzzer in the ninth row and bring him down; or she could turn on her heel and walk away – to go and fizz Debra an Alka-Seltzer and think through some other way to get at Trevor Benjamin, go back to her own survivor's life. The next thing she did would take her one way, or the other; like an emperor in the Coliseum she would decide whether that scum gang-boss lived or died – and whether or not she ran the risk of ruining her own life.

It was her father who decided her; those same thoughts she'd had about him before. If Benjamin behaved himself inside he could be back on the streets years before her dad ever saw the parole people: because Jonny Long would never keep hold of his rag for five years. And she could just see Benjamin ruling the roost meanwhile in Belmarsh, getting the drugs in, being the baron – his sort went round the estates boasting how much they liked prison food.

Before she knew it she had pressed the button; and to her surprise, straight off, Benjamin was there, coming round the corner of the stairwell. A jump ahead.

'Am-ba!'

'Tre-vor!' He didn't look at all dressed up to go out. He looked more . . . nondescript; not even his long patterned shirt.

267

'Lissn. I'm thinkin'. You an' me. We're gonna get it togever, yeah? You wanna be a gang wife, right? Come for initiation?'

'Right'. What was this? Where was he going? Amber took a step away from him.

'An' to get in the mood, you like to dance?'

'To feel relaxed. Dancing relaxes me; helps me bend and move; a dose of good jazz an' a nice dance really gets me going . . '. He was stepping towards her, and to back up what she was saying she had to step towards him. *Connor, why couldn't I have been ready with the knife?*

'Well, sister, I've got all that laid on upstairs. No need for buses an' walking the drags o' Woolwich'. And with a dancer's agility he suddenly threw an arm around her waist and spun her into the lift – whose doors were fixed open, waiting.

Shit! This wasn't how she'd planned it. It was her who was supposed to pull the surprise, not Trevor Benjamin – still holding her too tightly, too frontally, as the lift took them up to the ninth floor, his ugly lips in her face. Now she'd got to think again. Now she'd got to kill him in his flat; or plan to do it somewhere else another time. She closed her eyes, looking like passion; but because by then he'd have made her his gang wife: and she'd stick that knife in herself before that ever happened. Oh, God! What was she going to do?

*

Sunil Dhillon stood his scooter on its stand at the entrance to Bartram House. He briefly pushed the flat button to alert Amber, but straight after he tapped in the entry numbers she'd given him, and as the door gave he walked on in. Beneath his scooter coat he was obeying the dress code printed on the awards invitation: 'smart casual', wearing a white silk 'grandad' shirt and a black linen suit, with patent leather shoes. He lifted the spare helmet to look at his watch as he waited for the lift door to open. Seven o'clock – about right for the eight o'clock start in Piccadilly – and coming onto Amber's balcony from the lift he tapped a little dance as he went along to her door.

To stand there flat-footed as no answer came to his knock. He gave ample time for her to get to the door, then he knocked again. And again. With a puzzled look on his face, he turned towards the view of a full silvery river in the evening light, the tide high on the turn. He rang once more, and was fumbling for his mobile phone beneath his coat somewhere when the door opened a crack.

'Wha'?'

It was Amber's mother, her nicotined mouth round the door.

'Sorry. Is Amber in, Mrs . . .'

Debra Long turned inwards to check – and to shout, 'Am-ber? Am-ber?' She took a couple of steps back along the passage and banged open the door of

Amber's bedroom. 'Am-ber!' – before she dragged herself back to Sunil on the balcony. 'Not in,' she told him.

'Not in?'

Debra simply stared back. 'Gone out again.'

'Again?'

'Out Friday, out tonight.'

'Where?'

'Gawd knows.' She squinted at him. 'Who are you, anyhow, wanting to know?'

'I'm a friend she was going to come out with.'

'Are you?' Debra found a smile. 'Well, she's stood you up, ain't she?'

'Looks like it.'

'Funny girl.' A thought suddenly seemed to come. 'Here, let's see how much money she's nicked this time ...'

Sunil frowned. How could that tell them anything?

Debra returned with a jar, counting a few notes. 'Another tenner, that's all. So she's local, boy. Local, somewhere. Could've had thirty.' But now she pulled out a scrap of paper. 'Straight as a carrot, though, that one. Leaves me a note where the money was ...'

'What's it say?' Sunil asked, exasperated. Debra uncreased it. He took it from her. It read, *'Borrowed for Connor.'*

'Why would she write that tonight?' he asked.

'Dunno. She never tells me nothing.'

'Was she dressed for . . . anything?' Sunil showed his own smart suit.

Debra shrugged, and sniffed.

'OK, thank you very much.' Sunil walked away, no dance in his step as he returned to the lift. Amber Long. Poor kid. A pushy mother was so much better than no mother. The door to the flat shut behind him with a clatter. He opened the lift, which was still on that floor: no Amber standing beautiful inside it – who could have gone down by the stairs while he came up. Wherever she was, Sunil Dhillon wasn't in her plans tonight.

'*Tatti!*' he swore.

'You look banana,' Benjamin told Amber as he took her along to his flat.

'Ta.' *But she didn't feel that way. She felt like a fly going into the spider's web.* She dragged her feet.

'Move your ass, then,' he said. 'Just 'ere. Let's get you a slug, then we'll 'ave all that jazz . . .' And with her shoulder bag arm pinned to her side he led her through the open door, into the empty flat that was waiting for them. 'Me mum's moved out,' he said, 'hubba-hubba! – got it to ourselves.'

'Lovely,' Amber managed. And in she went, not so much walking as guided. Pushed, even.

Sunil unstepped his scooter and fixed the spare helmet to the rear pillion. He wheeled the Lambretta to where he could get a clear push off between the flats: but just before he kicked at the pedal and twisted the throttle he squeezed instead at the brakes and pulled out his mobile phone. In went Amber's number, which rang for a while before her voicemail came on: and the Samsung was hardly shut when he had third thoughts – and he rang another number.

'Something's not right. Amber Long was coming out with me tonight – but she's gone off somewhere. She's a funny kid,' he told Ian Webber, 'but she wouldn't just blow me out. There's stuff going on, something she's doing for Connor – she left a note in her mother's jar, a sort of IOU. I was wondering, can you get a location? Ask your people to ring her number and get a fix?'

'You stay there,' Webber said. 'I'll get back to you.'

Trevor Benjamin's flat was familiar – and yet it wasn't. It had the same layout as Amber's, all the rooms in the same places, but with its swirling interior of Caribbean colours and its heavy furniture, it seemed both lighter and smaller at the same time. And it smelt exotic. She was looking at it all from a luxury leather armchair in the sitting room; a low seat which meant that for comfort her legs had to be either stretched out straight, or knees high in the air. Benjamin was sitting across from her in the opposite armchair, tapping his fingers on the leather, no question of dancing to the music he'd put on; which wasn't jazz but hip-hop; him looking at her as if he was waiting for her to take off her small cardigan to show her sparkly shoulders and her low neckline. He clunked the ice around in his Jack Daniels – and drank it like some pathetic imitation of James Bond, his fingers splayed. Not that he looked the part at all, in toecap boots and a sweater: more ready for the street than the bedroom.

This was it, then. He was thinking he was going to get his way, short cut, trying to get her in the mood with alcohol in her Coke; she could taste it. She sipped, and winked across the room at him. Well, two were playing the get-ready game – she was as sure as she could be that no one had seen her meet him downstairs; and it was going to be an easy grab for the knife she'd slid down the side of the cushion when the vermin had got her the drink.

'So, what you reckon 'appened to your bruvver?' he suddenly asked. He might want to get her into the bedroom, but he didn't seem in any hurry – which suited Amber, because if she did what she was going to do it was going to be done in here, not on his bed. She was tensed and primed for it. When he brought her the next drink he'd have to bend over to hand it to her – and that would be the moment. She'd stick him.

'Don't know. He fell, didn't he?'

'Good littl'un, he was. Real Crew.'

The scum-bag two-faced villain.

'Brill climber,' Benjamin said.

'Yeah, he could have whizzed up Everest if he'd ever got older.'

Benjamin was staring at her, looking as if he could see through her to the knife down the side of the chair. She shifted a fraction, her hand feeling for it, and diverted his attention towards a big picture on the wall – hung low, to match the low furniture.

'Nice picture.'

'Flowers. Golden Trumpet, what you're lookin' at,' he said. 'The ol' lady's fave from Kingston Town.' His pudgy nose twitched as if the blooms gave him hay fever.

The picture looked like an original, Amber could see the paint glinting, ridged up the way Van Gogh did it with his sunflowers, except the whole frame, bigger than the HD television, was filled with bright yellow blooms, no vase, no stalks. It reminded her of another place filled with yellow flowers; and that other world suddenly came into the room. Trent Park.

Which was when she thought she heard it in the gap between hip-hop tracks; a sound like a muffled cough, and not from outside. She went rigid, and her hand came off the knife.

'What's that? Is that someone?' She twisted in her seat.

'The ol' man along the landin'. Who else would it be? I told you, me mum's moved out.'

'Sounded like—' But Benjamin was on his feet and walking across the room towards her, frowning as he

274

stared. He picked up her glass from the low table and handed it to her. 'Drink up, Am-ba – you're in for a re-fill.'

Play for time. She had to be just right for this. 'So, are you going to tell me about being a Crew wife, then? Apart from the test?' The last word echoed on for ever: *test-test-test-test-test* . . .

'Rules. First you do as you're told – that's what you do.' Dead serious, he held her drink in front of her, his body nearer now, a great chance. 'Drink up, sis.'

Amber had to.

'Right. Same again?'

She could only nod.

He went, and feverishly Amber delved deeper – locating the knife at last, nearly cutting herself with it. She brought it up, had it ready – he'd have to come close again to give her the next drink – but now she found she couldn't grip it properly.

But, couldn't – or wouldn't?

Which was almost her last rational thought; because the walls began to spin around her, slowly at first, then faster, taking her stomach with them; she opened her eyes wide and stared straight ahead to try to stop this frightening thing that was happening. But instead of focusing, the swirling was drawing, drawing, drawing her to the picture of the flowers, hypnotising her to it, the flowers dancing before her eyes as if in a slight breeze, like, like . . . that other place she wanted to be

. . . where there was freedom . . . and girls laughed.

She tried with every last ounce of control to cling on to what was real; the world was rubber, she felt too whoozy, she was going under, her insides dropping like the big scream on a terror-ride. God, why couldn't she have . . . ? She dropped the knife and gripped hard at the arms of the chair to keep herself in this real place. But that picture was still moving, differently now; the flowers still swayed, but the scene was coming closer and closer, until all she could see were yellow trumpets. And suddenly she was there, going into that other place. In a flash of clarity she was back in that park, near that college, with the millions of daffodils; she actually heard those girls laughing . . . And there, tilting on the path that was twisting up and round beneath her, she knew for sure where she was heading. The room was filled with hip hop, but what she heard in her head was the Half Past Yesterday hit song wailing – 'No Way to Go'; the words swelling up and down as lights needled in her eyes: *No way to go for a girl like me* . . . And through the mists the truth reached out to hit her – listen to the words of the song – this wasn't any way to go. Trevor Benjamin wasn't worth the sacrifice. The way to go was . . . that . . . other . . . sort . . . of . . . real . . .

And the last thing she heard was her own loud, snoring, snort.

Chapter Twenty-three

'She had the blade down the side of the chair', Trevor Benjamin told his brother. 'Saw the silly bitch shove it.'

'Said she was trouble', Denny told him. 'She was gonna shank you.'

'Well, she won't now, will she?'

A mobile phone rang – and they each checked their own.

'Leave it. It's 'er's in 'er bag. Leave ev'rything, like, nach.'

The phone stopped.

'Get the needle an' the bottle. She'll be well in la-la land when she don' come round . . .' Trevor Benjamin laughed; and this time it sounded as if he meant it. His brother went out of the room. Trevor called through to him. 'You got the van?'

'Got it.'

'Got the carpet?' Trevor swung Amber's legs round and straightened her out.

'Out of a skip . . .' Denny Benjamin came back to the sitting room with a syringe, tapping the needle like some caring nurse. 'Not got a lot of "H", he said, 'but enough to keep 'er out of it; let the river do the rest . . .'

'Ringed your plates, have you – no one can't trace it if we get seen?'

''Course.'

'Make more 'oles wi' that sharp, like she's a reg'lar user. Then it's down through the Arsenal to the river while the tide's still runnin' out – an' then . . .'

'Splash,' said Denny – as he pushed Amber's cardigan up her arm, and put the needle to her skin.

''Appy dreams, slut,' said Trevor.

The Midnight Express van with the Benjamin brothers in the front and a rolled carpet in the back headed towards the Arsenal development along the River Thames, mostly housing now, both in the old, listed, armaments buildings and in modern flats.

'Get us up as near the ferry as you can,' Trevor commanded. 'It's all offices there, no nosy buggers on their little balconies.'

'No prob.'

And the pair of them started singing.

'Ol' man river, tha' ol' man river . . .'

'I ever told you, bro, you got a junk voice?'

'Yeah – an' it's gonna sing *"Kiss the junkie goo'bye . . .",'* Trevor crooned, before they both started getting high on nervous laughter.

*

Liz Kwayana was lead officer on duty at Thames Reach police station; and if she wasn't best pleased to get a request from a DC who was on his Sunday night off, she had sense enough to know that she should do something about it. Webber had been insistent that this could be serious; and he had the ear of Detective Superintendent Brewer. She was also a professional, and if a vulnerable kid like the sister of the dead boy from the Barrier Estate was in some sort of trouble, then she should take action. Within moments she was on to the Orange phone people, giving them the mobile number she'd got from Webber – with the authorisation code necessary for them to do a satellite fix on behalf of the Met.

'Keep me posted', she said. And she did the other thing Webber had requested: she informed Mr Brewer, and she had a car and two uniformed officers brought round to the front of the police station.

Lying deep in her shoulder bag Amber's phone was well muffled, rolled up with her inside the carpet. But the van was in the quietness of the Arsenal development, and Trevor Benjamin jerked his head.

'That poxy phone! I'm sure I 'eard that phone!'

'It's 'er nex' punter', Denny laughed. 'Wun'drin when she's gonna get to him . . .'

'Soon!' Trevor said. 'She'll soon be where she's goin'!'

The van was heading for the river down Charlie Lewis

Way, dodging through the public car park and over a flower bed to avoid the roadway barriers that kept the Arsenal residents safe from the likes of the Benjamins. Denny had done a good reconaissance. 'Down there. Foller roun' that building.'

There was no one about. The river was empty of boats, the last visitors to the Arsenal museums had long gone, and the Woolwich Free Ferry, five hundred metres upriver, had finished its Sunday roster. The sun had set, the moon not yet risen. Skirting between the empty office buildings, the van bumped over cobbles and came to a stop a few metres from the river railings that separated the Thames walkway from the ebbing tide.

'There's steps down to the wa'er,' Denny said, pulling on the handbrake.

'Let's get her out an' done with it. I wan' me dinner . . .'

'The poor little addik.' Denny punched Trevor's shoulder in triumph. 'Arm stuck with 'oles and on the game to pay for it – crap state some o' these janes get theirselfs into . . .'

'Make you right. Come on, then.'

And the pair of them went round to the rear doors of the van – only the sounds of Trevor's boots and the water hitting the flood wall disturbing the peace.

*

Choked by foul-smelling fibres and swaddled in their fabric, Amber tried to open her eyes. But they stung her when she did, and the never-ending bumping of her head pained her neck. Where was she? And *what* was she – alive, or dead? Was this dying, this thing happening to her? Had Connor had this? If it was, she wanted it over, quick. The wild thought vanished when she was suddenly sick, bile retching in her throat; and a weird lifting movement beneath her threw her head another way and her gullet was cleared. She tried to move her body, to wriggle, to move out of this stinking tunnel – but she was fixed tight with just enough space for her head to loll a little, this way and that, and she started to go back into that death again, and no frantic clutching with her fingers seemed to hold her from it.

'We've had three fixes,' Liz Kwayana told Ian Webber through his Bluetooth as he raced up the A2, his portable blue flashing. 'Barrier Estate – she was still there at first, then on Woolwich Road – and now she's in the Arsenal buildings.'

'Right.'

'And moving fast.'

'Where are you?'

'In a squad car. But there was an anti-racism festival at the Valley – Charlton Athletic; they're all coming out – we're trying to siren through. I'll get back to you.'

*

The heavy carpet was out of the back of the van, lying like a tree trunk on the cobbles. Trevor Benjamin ran up the steps to the Thames path. He looked over the railings at the high river and the swirl of strong currents; and he twisted back to stare all around him for any signs of human life. He whistled back to Denny. 'It's a "go"!' he hissed. 'Get 'er out!'

'She *is* out!'

'Out of the carpet, stupid!'

'Yeah . . .'

Trevor came running back, to give his brother a hand with Amber Long's unconscious body. 'Peach, wasn't she?' he said when he saw her upturned face. 'Forgettin' the sick.'

'She was. *Was.*' Denny took a quick look. 'They all look better, asleep.' And he pulled the carpet from under her.

Sunil's phone rang. 'Sunil Dhillon.'

'Webber. She's somewhere on the Arsenal land. Gone there very fast from the Barrier . . .'

'Where are you?'

'Dartford Heath – coming up the A2. Listen – our squad car's stuck in traffic. Can you get to the Arsenal on your scooter?'

'Right.' Immediately, Sunil cut his phone off; didn't bother with his helmet. He kick-started the Lambretta, and put his head down to weave through cars towards the ferry, and the Woolwich Arsenal.

Amber was out of the carpet, lying on the cobbles with her skirt up and her shoulder bag round her neck, almost throttling any last life out of her.

Trevor Benjamin stared at the sight of the limp limbs, white in the dusk, his face twisting in a pout. 'I could've had 'er, first,' he said ruefully.

'Never mind that, take her shoulders – I'll take the legs. Get her over the wall an' in that water.' Denny bent to her, as the mobile phone in her shoulder bag rang again; one ring, before cutting off.

'No answer,' Trevor said. 'An' there won't be, bitch, for a long, long, time.'

'Switched off,' added Denny. 'Gone dead.'

'Thames Path,' Liz Kwayana relayed to her driver from her iPhone. 'Coastguard site ref. GR one-two-two.'

'Where's that?'

'Keep going,' she commanded, 'the Yard are checking . . .'

Sunil Dhillon turned on to the Arsenal housing development. But it was a huge area: where would he start looking for Amber here; she could be in a vehicle of some sort – or already up in someone's flat. It would be like one man searching a small town. He stopped and sat straddled, his feet balancing the scooter as he looked around him. It was all offices where he was. He turned his handlebars away from them just as his mobile rang again.

'Sunil.'

'We've got a fix,' Webber told him. 'The sea wall. The nearest Arsenal land west before you come to the Woolwich Ferry. There's a red coastguard sign . . .'

'The sea wall!'

'Where are you?'

'Not far. I'll get down there . . .'

'Then leg it, Sunil – someone's up to no bloody good.'

But Sunil was already on his way, speeding through the wide spaces between the Arsenal buildings.

She could see stars, swirling above her; she could feel arms carrying her, like lifting her to offer her up to them. And Amber Long knew that she was going to heaven. On her lips was one word, which she repeated over and over. It was a name. *'Connor, Connor, Connor . . .'* It was hard to breathe, and she closed her eyes, turned her head aside. She had been a sister to him, and she would be judged for being that; she need not be afraid. And with a weak smile on her face, she felt the darkness come down again.

'Gawd, they're 'eavy when they're freaked out!'

Her body sagging in a 'u' shape, Amber was being carried from the cobbled roadway up to the Thames riverside walk, the tide ebbing on the other side of grey railings. Within seconds she and the Benjamins would be out of sight of anyone, on their way down the steps leading to the swirling waters. When:

'Oi! You! Stop! Stop!' Someone was running towards them, shouting loud enough to wake the Arsenal dead.

Trevor's head was up. 'Hit him!' he commanded Denny. 'Hit him! An' quick!'

Denny dropped Amber's legs and started to run at this man, ready with one great right fist to smash in the spoiler's face. But Sunil Dhillon was smaller, lighter on his feet, and as he ran and he shouted he dodged the first mighty punch and ran under it, put everything into reaching that other man who was dragging a girl towards the river.

'Amber! Amber!' he shouted. 'Fight 'em! Struggle! You stop that!' he screeched. He saw the man turn, hesitate . . .

When, smack! – two things happened. He was felled by a blow like a brick to the back of his head. And a police siren wailed, coming nearer and nearer.

Which Sunil did not hear. He was lying unconscious on the ground, as helpless as Amber Long.

But when he came round, Ian Webber was there, and so were the police – and an ambulance with its doors open bustling with paramedics. And there, too, was a police van into the back of which two men were being hefted.

In all the confusion and the ringing in his head, Sunil

could just make out what Webber was saying.

'Great stuff, Sunil. You bought a few seconds; and Benjamin couldn't do it on his own in time. Attempted murder – how's that for starters? Won't that get some Crew talking . . .?' Which was a great congratulation to hear – before Sunil suddenly vomited all over the heritage cobbles.

Which marked the start of two days' sick leave for him – both of them spent at the hospital bedside of Amber Long after touch-and-go emergency treatment for respiratory arrest. But whose smile, when she woke and recognised him, was as 'A-star' as anyone could ever wish to see.

'Sunil . . .'

'Amber . . .'

'What happened?'

'Trevor Benjamin. Tried to drug you, and drown you. But we didn't let that happen.'

She tried to pull herself up. 'We?'

'People who care about you . . .'

'Like, you?'

'Like me. And the police.'

Amber smiled again, and reached out a hand to touch his neck. It was getting better. 'I wasn't going to do it,' she said. 'I changed my mind.'

'I'm pleased. Webber thinks he'll get thirty years for what he did.'

'I bet your mum's proud of you now.'

He laughed, too. 'I think she is.'

'Tell her I'll come round and see her soon.' She opened her droopy lids again. 'So she can cook me one of her famous . . .' Her voice was tailing off.

'Chicken madras,' Sunil finished, as he leaned over to kiss her on the forehead.

The kiss brought her back. 'Because . . . you know . . . I found out . . . which way I want to go.' She stroked his hand. 'It's your way, Sunil Dhillon. And I'll tell you . . . where . . . I'm . . . going.'

He looked deeply into her eyes. 'I think I know,' he said.

'I'm going to . . .Trent . . .' she started.

'. . . Park,' he finished. But by then she was sleeping peacefully again.

No Way To Go is Bernard Ashley's 21st novel
Here is a full list of all 21 titles:

No Way To Go ISBN: 978 1 40830 239 2	**Orchard Books**	**(2009)**
Solitaire	Usborne Publishing	(2008)
Flashpoint ISBN: 978 1 84616 060 8	**Orchard Books**	**(2007)**
Down to the Wire ISBN: 978 1 84616 965 6	**Orchard Books**	**(2006)**
Smokescreen	Usborne Publishing	(2006)
Ten Days to Zero ISBN: 978 1 84616 957 1	**Orchard Books**	**(2005)**
Freedom Flight	Orchard Books	(2003)
Revenge House	Orchard Books	(2002)
Little Soldier ISBN: 978 1 86039 879 7	**Orchard Books**	**(1999)**
Tiger Without Teeth	Orchard Books	(1998)
Johnnie's Blitz	Viking Books	(1995)
Bad Blood	Julia MacRae Books	(1988)
Running Scared	Julia MacRae Books	(1986)
Janey	Julia MacRae Books	(1985)
High Pavement Blues	Julia MacRae Books	(1983)
Dodgem	Julia MacRae Books	(1982)
Break in the Sun	Oxford University Press	(1980)
A Kind of Wild Justice	Oxford University Press	(1978)
All My Men	Oxford University Press	(1977)
Terry on the Fence	Oxford University Press	(1975)
The Trouble with Donovan Croft	Oxford University Press	(1974)

The titles in bold are available to purchase from Orchard Books.
Orchard books are available from all good bookshops, or can be ordered direct from the
publisher: Orchard Books, PO BOX 29, Douglas IM99 1BQ
Credit card orders please telephone 01624 836000 or fax 01624 837033
or visit our website: www.orchardbooks.co.uk or email:
bookshop@enterprise.net for details.
To order please quote title, author and ISBN and your full name and address.
Cheques and postal orders should be made payable to 'Bookpost plc.'
Postage and packing is FREE within the UK (overseas customers
should add £1.00 per book).